WOEBEGONE

The town of Woebegone barely survived on its cattle market trade. Then, Doug Sanders, a Los Angeles buyer, arrived. A deal was struck, the steers were sold and the money lodged at the bank. However, Jasper Dent and Wild Man Bore had shadowed the herd for the last four days. They knew that where there were cows there was money. Trouble wasn't slow in coming and it was up to Sheriff Tom Hilks to sort it all out.

Books by D D Lang
in the Linford Western Library:

LAST STOP LIBERTY

CP/48

D D LANG

WOEBEGONE

Complete and Unabridged

LINFORD
Leicester

First published in Great Britain in 1997 by
Robert Hale Limited
London

First Linford Edition
published 1998
by arrangement with
Robert Hale Limited
London

British Library CIP Data

Lang, D D, *1948*–
   Woebegone.—Large print ed.—
Linford western library
1. Western stories
2. Large type books
I. Title
823.9′14 [F]

ISBN 0–7089–5198–8

Published by
F. A. Thorpe (Publishing) Ltd.
Anstey, Leicestershire

Set by Words & Graphics Ltd.
Anstey, Leicestershire
Printed and bound in Great Britain by
T. J. International Ltd., Padstow, Cornwall

This book is printed on acid-free paper

To my children
Leah and Ben, with love

1

JASPER DENT and Wild Man Bore sat outside the First Bank of Woebegone, a small town that clung perilously to the edge of the vast Nevada desert.

They both watched as a besuited man, doffing his hat to both men and women who walked past on the boardwalk, took out a bunch of keys from his coat pocket and, after selecting the right key, opened the double doors of the bank and swiftly entered, closing the doors behind him.

A woman knocked on the bank door and the same man opened it to let her in, closing the door once again.

The two men waited.

Three minutes later, two more people arrived, one male the other female, and they were let into the bank. The door remained closed, presumably locked on the inside. The day's business was about to commence.

Dent and Bore had followed the cattle drive for three weeks, waiting to see where it bedded down, for they both knew that cattle meant money. Money was the one thing they were a mite short of and they aimed to put that to rights.

Dent checked his pocketwatch: nine o'clock on the button, exactly the same as the day before. The time between the manager opening up and the three members of staff arriving was four minutes. Within a minute of yesterday's time.

Satisfied that the pattern was pretty consistent, Jasper Dent nodded to Bore and both men walked across the street to the small café that had been open since dawn.

"What'll it be, gents," the owner, Will Carlson asked.

"Coffee."

"Nothin' to eat?"

"Nope." Jasper Dent took out a long

cheroot and bit the end off, spitting it on the floor. He struck a match and lit up, sending a cloud of white smoke in the air and filling the small café with the smell of the phosphor from the hand-made match.

"We doin' it tomorrer?" Bore asked.

Dent didn't say a word. He just nodded.

The coffee arrived and Carlson placed two mugs on the table. Neither Dent nor Bore thanked him. Carlson went back to the kitchen. He knew better than to try and strike up a conversation with two men who obviously didn't want to talk.

Woebegone began to fill up. The drive had been in town for two days now, the cattle had been sold and some of the drovers had been hired to see the drive through to the market in Los Angeles, a journey of some two-hundred miles.

The money was in the bank as cash was still the order of the day. Dent knew that the hands had been given money to see them over the first couple of nights' drinking, but that their wages would be paid the next day at noon.

Dent threw two bits on the table and they left the café. Carlson watched as they pushed through the front door, leaving it open. He didn't like the looks of those two men, but he had no time to dwell on the subject as people began to clamour for their breakfasts. Carlson closed the door, trying to keep as much dust out of the place as he could; a battle he lost daily.

★ ★ ★

Sheriff Tom Hilks had had a busy couple of nights. Two shootings, but mainly drunks and fistfights. The drovers had to let off steam and, as there was no official whorehouse, beer and whiskey was their natural outlet.

The small jailhouse was full to busting and Tom grabbed a bunch of keys hanging on a nail by his desk and proceeded to release the overnight

4

prisoners. The cells to the rear of his office stank to high heaven, and Tom knew he'd have to get old Charlie, the town's odd-job-man, to sluice the place out.

It seemed that what the men had drunk the night before had more than doubled on the cell floor. The piss-bucket was overflowing and Tom held his nose as he unlocked the cell door and stepped back to set them free.

The cell, designed to hold two men, held seven. Seven hangovers and fourteen red eyes stared at him and slowly the men got to their feet, looking somewhat sheepish. Not that they could remember what they were in jail for.

"Two dollars a head," Tom said, "cash money, an' then git outta here."

The men fished in their pockets and managed to scrape fourteen dollars together.

"An' I don't wanna see you back in here tonight," Tom said as he collected the money.

"You won't, Sheriff," one of the men answered.

Tom watched as they filed out into the bright sun, he knew that whatever aches and pains they had would double as the sunlight hit their eyeballs and that it'd take the rest of the day for them to start feeling even half-way human again.

Tom smiled to himself as he deposited the fine money in the top drawer of his desk. At least, he thought, the mayor wouldn't be on his back about feeding the prisoners breakfast on council money, even though Will Carlson would be disappointed at the loss of seven meals.

Tom left the jailhouse in search of Charlie; the old man would be glad of a dollar to clean up the cells, and Tom would be glad of a coffee.

★ ★ ★

Henry Warton had been manager of the First Bank of Woebegone, so named as it was the first, and only, bank the town had, for six months. Transferred from Boston, where he was used to the fine city life, Henry had not taken to the West at all.

As far as he was concerned, most of the townsfolk, with one or two exceptions, were barbarians, and he tried to come into contact with them as little as possible. Consequently, he was not a popular man as most people thought him too big for his britches and, given half the chance, there were quite a few men who'd willingly take him down a peg or two.

Henry sat at his overly-large mahogany desk, the high-backed leather chair squeaked as he shifted his weight, opening the centre drawer of the desk and selecting his paperwork for the morning. Henry's life consisted of paperwork, everything was done by the book, without exception.

The staff, trained by Henry himself, set about their business, waiting for the time-lock to click open on the giant safe, shipped from Boston by buckboard at considerable expense, so they could fill up their cash-drawers and start the day's trading.

As usual, one or two people stood outside the glass-paned door, waiting for the bank to open. They knew that Henry Warton wouldn't unlock the door until nine-thirty; not a minute earlier, not a minute later. But they still waited.

Inside, Henry surveyed the bank: it was small, too small for Henry. He didn't even have a private office. His desk, chair and two large filing cabinets filled one quarter of the office space, the giant safe to his left, the cash-counter to his right.

Three tills were open and ready to be filled. The metallic clunk made him turn his head as the lock clicked. Henry took his pocketwatch out; nine-twenty-five. The three tellers stood in a neat line, each holding a wooden cash-tray, their eyes on Henry Warton.

He stood, replaced his pocketwatch,

took out two large keys and walked to the safe door. He inserted one key and turned it, hearing as he did so the reassuring smoothness of the tumblers falling into place with precision. Then he inserted the second key and turned that in the opposite direction. More tumblers set inside the nine-inch-thick door slid smoothly into position.

Henry took both keys out and replaced them in his vest pocket. Then, holding the brass handle that protruded from the black-painted safe door, he slid it downwards. Four bolts slid smoothly back inside the door and Henry pulled the safe open.

It was nine-twenty-eight.

Inside the safe, on a shelf to the right, were three wooden trays, each neatly stacked with folding money and change. These trays fitted into the trays the tellers held. Henry retrieved them, one by one, the tellers returned to the counter and sat, backs straight, hands on laps.

The tellers had balanced from the

previous day and carefully counted out the float money, so all they had to do was wait for the doors to open.

Henry walked to the double doors and took his pocketwatch out again: nine twenty-nine. He watched as the second hand slowly made its way round and at precisely nine-thirty, he opened the doors.

★ ★ ★

Dent and Bore stood on the opposite side of the street and watched as the blind went up and the double doors opened inwards. The four people waiting outside entered and the doors were closed.

The bank was open.

Dent had deposited five dollars when he'd opened an account the day before and in the time it took to organize the paperwork, he'd had a good look round. The layout of the bank was indelibly imprinted on his brain, he felt as if he could walk round it blindfold.

The safe door had been open, as was Henry Warton's custom, and Dent's mouth had watered as he studied the money-bags he could see from the counter.

His palms had itched and it was all he could do to stop himself taking out his sideiron and holding up the bank there and then.

But there were too many people around and for once Dent curbed his natural impetuosity, smiled as the teller handed him a receipt for his five dollars, almost all the money they had between them, and left.

But not for long.

Jasper Dent entered the bank three more times that day, on the last occasion to withdraw his five dollars, but he made sure he was served by a different teller.

They had a day to waste and Woebegone was no town for excitement. There was nothing to do but drink, and with only five dollars, they couldn't do much of that; still, they'd drink their money away first and then look around town, maybe even take a ride out to survey the surrounding area.

Dent had met Bore in Fort Worth, Texas. Both men were in their early twenties then, now, approaching mid-forty, they were inseparable.

Dent had saved Bore's life — accidentally as it turned out. The bar they were both in was crowded, it was Saturday night and over seventy people were in there intent on drinking themselves into a stupor as quickly as they could.

Bore, alone at the end of the bar, caught the eye of a cowboy who took exception to the man looking at him.

What started out as a fist-fight in the dirt, turned into gunplay as the cowboy's partners joined in the fray.

Jasper Dent had just ridden into town and was dismounting when a stray bullet hit the hitching post he was tying his horse to. Jasper Dent did not like that one bit.

Bore was surrounded by four cowboys,

guns drawn and levelled at the man. Jasper Dent thought the odds a little short and decided to lend a hand, or rather, his gun.

Making his way to Bore's side the two men stood and faced the four cowboys.

Dent could tell the cowboys were drunk and he smiled, a steel-cold glint in his eyes which almost sobered up the four men. Unfortunately for them, it didn't sober them up enough.

Without preamble, Dent drew and fired four times. The surprised looks on the men's faces as their own guns went off involuntarily, firing slugs harmlessly into the dirt as they fell, was a look Dent had seen many times before.

If only the four men had paid a little more attention they might still be alive. They didn't see Dent's low-slung holster, tied to his thigh with a leather thong. They couldn't have seen the wooden handle of his revolver, if they had, they'd've apologized and bought the men a beer.

The Colt's handle had so many notches in it it was a wonder Dent's hand wasn't full of splinters.

Wild Man Bore swallowed hard, his gun was still holstered. As the smoke settled, there were four dead men lying in the dirt forming pools of blood.

The marshal of Fort Worth was on the scene in seconds, but four onto two, and eye-witnesses cleared Dent of any blame.

For twenty years the two men had ridden a trail of death and destruction across the mid-west before arriving in Woebegone where they aimed to create more havoc.

The day was to be long one, both men knew that, and it didn't help matters when after an hour they were once again penniless and not even drunk.

"We gotta git ourselves some pocket-money," Dent said.

"How're we gonna do that?" Bore asked.

"Time we had a real good look

around this town," Dent replied and pulled out his last cheroot.

The saloon was practically empty as they drained their glasses.

"We could always help ourselves to the bartakings," Bore said.

"Nope. Too damn obvious. We gotta get cash from somewhere's a mite quieter, someplace we ain't spent no time," Dent said. "Come on, let's go looksee."

The two men rose and ambled out of the saloon into the dusty, hot air of Woebegone.

Like most small towns, Woebegone had a main street and precious little else. Few people lived in town, most had small homesteads on the perimeter, some even lived in makeshift tents. The liveryman and the barkeep, along with the café owner and the sheriff, were the only permanent residents.

From the saloon, the layout of the town was pretty much like a thousand other towns. No hotel, but there was a bunkhouse for the hands too drunk to get back to their ranches and not drunk enough to get slapped in the jailhouse; a general store which sold anything and everything and bartered for most things trappers brought into town.

The livery stable was one of the biggest buildings as, to the rear, was the stockade where the steers were bought and sold. Clem Watkins and his sidekick Crooked Grin, a full-blooded Apache Clem had found as a boy and treated as his own son ever since, ran the place between them. Grooming, shoe-making and feed, made them a comfortable living.

The jailhouse came next, a small, wooden building big enough for an office, the cell and a place for Tom Hilks to bed down. The café, and two houses were set further back. One belonged to the storekeeper and his wife; the other was empty, had been since the previous owner, Walter McCabe, had died in his sleep. It had taken three weeks before anyone found his body and by that time there wasn't much of Walter McCabe left to bury.

Jasper Dent and Wild Man Bore walked the length of the town and then back again.

"Shit!" Dent said and spat into the dirt. "There ain't nothin' here."

"What 'bout the store?" Bore said.

"Town's too damn small. Any shootin' an' everyone'll hear it. Let's take a ride."

They turned and walked across to the livery stable to retrieve their horses. Clem Watkins watched as they approached.

"Ready to leave?" he asked the two men.

"Nope. We's jus' goin' fer a ride, see what work we can pick us up," Dent said.

"That'll be fifty cents a horse," Watkins said.

"We ain't got fifty cents," Dent replied. "Leave you a gun, though, as a deposit."

"Let's see it," Watkins said.

Dent walked to his saddle and pulled

out a Winchester rifle and handed it to Watkins.

"Worth at least ten dollars," Dent said.

Watkins flicked the lever up and down, loading a slug into the breech. Then he aimed the long barrel skywards and pulled the trigger. The blast broke through the morning air like thunder and within a few seconds there must have been ten or twelve people rushing out to see what the fuss was all about.

"Rifle seems okay to me," Watkins said. "It'll do 'til you git some cash."

"Fair enough," Dent said and began to saddle up.

Mounted atop his mare Dent leaned down and said: "We'll be back afore sundown — 'less we ain't."

Watkins said nothing, just watched as the two men rode out of town. He stashed the rifle behind some hay bales, just in case they decided to sneak back and retrieve the weapon, and went about his business.

The day was, as ever, hot. Neither Dent nor Bore had washed, and their clothes were covered in sand and dirt, as were their beards that began to take shape after a week without shaving.

Within a hundred yards of leaving town, the silence descended on them like a cloak. There was no breeze, no rustling, the only noise was soft hoof sounds as their animals walked through the sandy trail that led they knew not where.

A mile or so further on they came across a shack. It seemed deserted. There was a neat little picket fence surrounding the property and a tended yard. A small barn was out back, big enough for a couple of horses and feed, but for precious little else.

They reined in their mounts and watched for any sign of life. No smoke came from the small stone chimney and the drapes were pulled tight closed.

"Go roun' the other side, see if you can see anyone," Dent said to Bore.

Without replying, Bore dug his heels

into the horse's flanks and walked on. Surveying the homestead from the other side, he called out: "Nothin' here."

Dent breathed out 'dang fool' to himself. Bore had shouted loud enough to wake the dead.

He dismounted and tied his animal to the picket fence, at the same time, he removed his Colt from its holster. Bore came across and joined him. They pushed open the small gate and walked down the gravel path towards the front door.

* * *

From her small kitchen set at the rear of the shack, Aggie Miller had heard the shout from outside. Instinctively, she reached for the rifle she kept hanging over the wood stove and loaded the chamber.

Alone now these past four years since her husband upped and went off with a trail drive never to return, she'd learned the art of caution where strangers were concerned.

At thirty years of age, Aggie was a stunner and half the men in town had tried to bed her on more than one occasion. The only success had been the sheriff, and he was still awaiting on the second time, even though she was sweet on him, and he knew it.

Aggie went to the front of the shack and, using the barrel of the rifle, she moved the drapes across just enough to see out.

Just as she saw the bearded figure of Jasper Dent, the front door burst open and there stood Wild Man Bore.

Aggie tried to level the rifle but Bore was too quick for her. In one swift move, he cuffed her and Aggie fell to the floor.

2

TOM HILKS sat in the café over his second cup of coffee. Old Charlie had been found and hired and, hopefully, was hard at work cleaning up the cell. Tom reckoned on having a peaceful day.

The gunshots almost made him drop the coffee mug.

Rushing outside, he was just in time to see two men ride off, a third, lying prone in the dirt, was the obvious recipient of the shots.

"Anyone see what happened?" Tom shouted as he ran towards the body.

A silence greeted his question.

The man, young, blond and dead, was unknown to Tom. Must be a drover, he thought.

A small knot of people gathered round the body. Two neatly drilled holes were clearly visible in the man's shirt.

"Any one see who did this?" Tom asked no one in particular.

"I see's two fellas," one of the townsfolk said. "Didn' recognize 'em. Not from round here." The man spat brown liquid into the dirt, the tell-tale bulge in his cheek told Tom he was chewing tobacco.

The man ambled off down the street without waiting for a response or even turning back.

"Someone get Bill out here," Tom asked and a man left the group to get the undertaker.

Tom went through the dead man's pockets but there was nothing to identify him. He found four dollar bills; at least, he thought, he had enough on him to pay for his own funeral.

There was little else Tom could do in the street, so he decided to trail the two riders. He couldn't prove the killing unlawful or otherwise, but he felt he'd better do something.

Tom saddled up and left Woebegone — he hoped not for long.

* * *

Doug Sanders was what most folks called a cattle baron. He didn't own a cattle ranch, he dealt in beef on the hoof. He was an expert at getting the right animals at the right price and then selling them on at a profit.

He had his fingers in so many pies it was a wonder he had time to dress each morning.

He stood now behind the livery stable, surveying the herd he'd just purchased. Some of the steers were scrawny, but that was to be expected. The last two days the herd had been driven across the desert, almost non-stop. Doug knew that, within a day or two, with some good feed and plenty of water, they'd fatten up some. Then he could drive them on to Los Angeles.

City folks out there bought all the beef steak he could supply, and Doug was only too pleased to supply it.

Doug had six armed men with him day and night. They guarded him, his money, and now his head. The twelve dollars a head he'd paid would turn into twenty, maybe twenty-five dollars a head by the time he reached the market-place in Anaheim, and even allowing for the drovers' pay, he still stood to make a mighty fine profit.

Doug was also a walking catalogue store. Whenever he visited these outlying markets, he always made sure he had enough goods to sell on.

Dresses and material for the ladies. Maybe some of the latest handguns and rifles for the men. Tin toys for the boys and dolls for the little girls. His wagon was stuffed fit to bulging with goods from pots and pans to tablecloths and leather boots to ladies' walking-out shoes, Stetsons to bonnets. You name it Doug Sanders had it, and if he didn't, he'd make sure he'd have it on his next visit.

The cattle were still calm and placid. The drive had taken it out of them and they stood in the stockade as peaceful as you like. Doug knew enough about steers to know that in two days' time, they'd start getting restless. And that's when fighting began. Animals could get killed or injured and that meant a loss in profits. Doug was anxious that that didn't happen.

He heard the shooting and watched as two riders galloped off into the desert. A smile played across his lips. He'd paid them well and they'd carried out the job he'd given them.

Sanders watched as the sheriff took off, no doubt, he thought, in pursuit of the two riders. But Doug Sanders wasn't concerned about that. He'd used the two men before. They knew their business and he knew they wouldn't be caught.

★ ★ ★

Aggie Miller opened her eyes and winced. Her jaw felt as if a bull steer had trampled on it. Her eyes came to rest on the leering face of Bore. His face was no more than six inches away from hers and she could tell by the look in his eyes that he wasn't concerned for her welfare.

From behind her there was movement. She tried to turn her head, but the bonds that bound her were tight and the whole lower half of her face ached.

The rough gag she had in her mouth was tight — too tight — and she knew her face was swelling up.

The man in front of her started rubbing her leg with one hand, the other hand was pressed into his own crotch. He licked his lips and a grin spread across his face, but didn't reach his eyes.

From behind her she heard plates and pots and pans being flung around. What were they looking for? Who were they? Those and many more questions flashed through her mind. Plus the thought: when would they rape her?

"Goddamnit," the man behind her shouted out in frustration. "Where d'ya keep the money?"

Aggie could only grunt.

"Take that goddamn gag off!" Dent shouted.

Bore grinned, revealing black and broken teeth, with the close proximity of his face, Aggie could smell his sour breath and the stink from his body. It almost made her retch.

Bore moved behind her and began untying the gag. The relief as it came loose was only tempered by the fact that Bore's hand slid down her chest and cupped one of her breasts — hard.

Unseen by Dent, Bore kept his hand there and there was nothing Aggie could do about it. He kept moving his hand in hard, tight circles and, despite herself, Aggie knew that her nipple was hardening. Worse, so did Bore.

"I said, where d'ya keep the money?" Dent rasped again.

"Table drawer. At the back," Aggie replied.

Bore's hand stopped moving, but he was still pressing himself tight up behind her.

"Get the hell away from her," Dent

said. "We got more important things to do than go messin' with her."

"You might have," Bore said, his voice had gone thick with lust.

Dent pulled the drawer out of the kitchen table, its contents fell to the floor. He picked up a small cotton bag and, pulling open the strings, inside he found thirty dollars.

"This it?" he said.

"That's all I have," Aggie replied. "Now get the hell out of my home!"

Dent laughed out loud, Bore followed suit. Then Dent noticed the unopened bottle of whiskey standing on a shelf.

He walked across the room and, for the first time, Aggie saw the face of the second man. He reached up and took a hold of the bottle. Pulling the cork out with his teeth he took a mighty swig of the brown liquid, then passed it on to Bore.

Taking his hand from Aggie's breast, Bore swiftly drank nearly half the contents, burped loudly and handed the bottle back to Dent.

"She's a purty one," Dent said, and took another swig of whiskey.

"She surely is," Bore agreed, and this time he used both his hands on Aggie's breasts, squeezing them tightly, a lascivious look on his dark face.

"Guess we's got time," Dent said.

"We sure have," Bore said. "We sure have."

* * *

The trail Hilks was following suddenly split into two. One veered east, the other west.

"Shit an' hell," he said to himself as he reined his animal in. He studied the landscape to his left and right. Nothing. No cloud dust, no noise. Nothing.

"Shit!"

Tom Hilks sat atop his horse for a few more minutes before deciding to head back to town. No sense in wasting time out here in the middle of nowhere.

Hilks reined his horse round, then

had a better idea. Heading west, he thought he'd pay Aggie a visit; he hadn't seen her for a couple of days, so he could pretend it was official, making sure she was all right. He grinned to himself and rode on.

★ ★ ★

Unbuckling his gunbelt, Dent had already decided on the pecking order. He was to be first.

"Gag her up agen, Bore," he said and took another swig of the whiskey.

Neither man had had a woman in more weeks than they could remember and this one sure would make a change from the highly-painted whores they were used to.

Dent handed the bottle to Bore. "Don't take too long," he said to Dent. "I ain't sure I can wait."

"Takes as long as it takes," Dent replied, the words slightly slurred through whiskey and animal lust.

Dent undid his jeans belt and started

31

undoing the fly buttons when the sound of an approaching rider filled his ears.

He froze.

The look of terror that filled Aggie's eyes was still there, but now she had hope in her heart.

Pulling his belt back on and picking up his gunbelt, Dent took out his Colt and edged his way to the draped window.

Two hundred yards away, he saw the rider riding straight towards the house.

"Hellfire!" he said under his breath.

"Who is it?" Bore asked.

"How the hell do I know. Some fella, is all. Comin' straight here."

"You expectin' anyone, missy?" Bore asked.

Aggie shook her head.

"We got time to scat," Dent said. "We can allus come back. Anytime."

Without a word being exchanged, the two men left the shack and ran for their horses. Mounting, they headed back towards Woebegone. At least they had enough money to see them through the day. Maybe even get a bed for the night.

Tom Hilks was lost in his thoughts as he approached Aggie's shack. The two riders, although not charging hell for leather, certainly weren't wasting any time in getting away. Tom reined in and, even though he was sheriff, it took a few seconds for him to realize that maybe Aggie was in trouble.

Kicking his horse he galloped on, reining in and jumping down in one swift movement. He ran straight into the house and found Aggie, still tied to the chair, a tear falling down her cheek. Even with the gag in, she smiled as she saw who had entered.

The second thing Tom noticed was the dirt on her dress. The dirt that surrounded both her breasts. Questions filled his head, but he put them to one side as he untied the ropes and released the gag from her mouth.

Aggie wept with relief as she stood and flung her arms around Tom's neck.

"Oh, Tom, I'm so glad you came over," she said, sobs racking her body.

Tom was silent for a while, content to hold her in his arms. As the sobs abated, he asked if she was all right.

"Yes, yes I'm fine. They were going to, going to . . . "

"I know, I know. But they didn't, did they?" he didn't mean for it to come out as a question, but the boiling rage he felt and the jealousy that filled him affected the statement.

Aggie pulled back slightly, her arms still round his neck, and looked him straight in the eye: "No," she said pointedly.

Tim grinned, feeling a blush colour his cheeks.

"When they heard you coming," she went on, "they said they could come back *any* time."

"Well, you ain't stayin' out here on your own," Tom said. "I'll get you fixed up in town, where I can keep an eye on you."

"I'd be obliged, Tom," she said.

"They took my savings, as well."

"How much?"

"All the money I have in the world, Tom. Thirty dollars."

"You ever seen 'em before?" he asked.

"No, never. And I hope I don't see them again."

"If you do," Tom added, "it'll be with me. I promise you that."

They held each other tightly for a few moments longer, before Tom told her to get her things together while he hitched up the buggy.

★ ★ ★

Dent and Bore reached town and immediately tethered their animals back at the livery stable. Dent gave Clem two dollars, one they owed and one for tonight. He was certain they wouldn't be in this neck of the woods after nine-thirty in the morning.

Clem Watkins handed back the rifle they'd left as a deposit. He was hoping

35

they wouldn't come back, the rifle was better than the money.

Dent and Bore called in the saloon and bought two bottles of rot-gut whiskey, then made their way to the bunkhouse. It was noon, so they hoped that most of the drovers would be out droving, or whatever it was they did. They both planned to lie low until tomorrow morning.

Inside the bunkhouse, Doug Sanders was issuing orders to his men about the drive that was due to head out west at one in the afternoon. He stopped mid-sentence as Dent and Bore entered.

He knew instinctively that the two men that had just entered were not cowhands. He looked at Dent's holster, saw the handle of the Colt and a sly grin licked at one side of his lips.

"You boys lookin' fer work?" he asked.

"Hell, no," Dent replied. "We're looking for a bed, a drink, some shut-eye an' then we're outta here."

Sanders finished giving orders to the

rest of his crew and sent them on their way. He turned to face Dent.

"I could use men like you," he said. "Not for cow-poking, either. I'm always lookin' for a good gun. Are you good with that gun?"

Instead of answering, Dent drew and had the barrel of the Colt under Sanders' neck quicker than the blink of an eye.

"What d'ya think, mister?" Dent asked.

"Seems to me," Sanders said, maintaining his cool, "you boys are exactly what I'm lookin' for."

"Yeah, well maybe, Mister City-Dude, you ain't what we's lookin' for," Bore said.

"Thousand dollars help change your mind?" Sanders said.

Dent lowered the Colt and reholstered it. "What you talkin' about, mister?"

"I'm talkin' about a thousand dollars — each," Sanders said.

"Yeah, sure," Dent flopped down on an empty bunk.

"'Less of course, you boys don't have no balls."

Dent pulled the cork out of the whiskey bottle and drew a slug: "We got balls, mister. You got two thousand dollars?"

Sanders went to put his left hand inside his jacket pocket. Quick as a rattler strike, Dent was up with his gun out again.

"Hold on," Sanders said. "You asked me a question. Now I'm gonna answer it." He pulled out his wallet and showed Dent the contents. "I'd say there was more'n two thousand dollars in there, wouldn't you?"

Dent whistled and put his gun away.

"What exactly we gotta do, mister," Bore asked.

"Plenty o' time for that, later." Sanders said. "I got some more people coming back pretty soon. Three more boys you're sure to get on with."

Sanders grinned at both men. Casually, he threw two brand-spanking-new hundred-dollar bills on the bunk.

"A sign of good faith," he said. "I'll see you both at nine tonight. Okay?"

Dent and Bore picked up a bill each. "You gotta deal, mister," Dent said and kissed the bill before stuffing it into his back pocket.

"Nine o'clock, here," Sanders said and started to leave.

Outside, Tom Hilks was riding shotgun on Aggie Miller's buggy. Dent pulled back when he saw the man's horse.

"You know the sheriff?" Sanders asked.

"Not exactly," Bore said. "We was gonna have some fun with the little lady when he showed up and we high-tailed it outta there."

"Did he see you?" Sanders asked.

"Nope. But she sure did." Dent pointed at the woman beside Hilks.

"Stay inside. I'll send another couple of bottles over," Sanders said. "Nine o'clock, gentleman." With that Sanders left the two men to the serious business of drinking.

Tom Hilks didn't see the two men inside the bunkhouse, but he tipped his hat as Sanders strode across the street, heading towards the saloon.

"Afternoon, Mr Sanders," Tom said.

"Sheriff," Sanders tipped his hat, "Ma'am."

Aggie nodded, but didn't speak.

Sanders continued his journey towards the saloon.

"He weren't one of 'em, was he Aggie?" Tom asked.

"Oh, now, Tom. Nothing like them. Nothing like them."

3

DOUG SANDERS' travelling catalogue store was doing a thriving business. Even at the best of times, Harold Meeks, the general store owner, could only manage to order goods and get them delivered in six to eight weeks. Here was Sanders with goods already in and ready to take away.

Of course, they were a mite expensive, but they were immediate.

The usual wrangling was taking place between customers, there was only so much you could cram into a covered wagon and inevitably more than one person wanted an item that was in short supply. Most of it was good humoured — up to a point — but a woman who'd set her sights on a bolt of material or a dress, was likely to be a damn sight feistier than one could imagine.

Sanders, of course, did not actually sell the items himself, he had a man hired for that job. Sanders sat in the saloon surrounded by his bodyguards, to all intents and purposes socializing. In fact, he was planning his next move.

Born and raised from poor stock on the outskirts of Los Angeles, he'd watched as his father, a hard working dirt-farmer, had toiled his life away to little avail. He'd died when he was forty, and Doug was expected to take over the sodbusting himself and continue the farm.

Doug Sanders had other ideas. Seeing his father die in poverty had had a bad effect on Sanders, not because his father was dead, that had little effect on him, it was because he was a loser. One thing that Doug determined as he stood by his father's grave, one hot sunny Sunday morning, with only his mother for company and a travelling pastor who officiated, was that Doug Sanders would *never* be a loser.

At the tender age of fourteen, he left his mother and home and walked the eighty miles to Los Angeles. He didn't have a clue as to what he'd do when he got there, but one thing was for sure, it wouldn't be sodbusting.

Spending the next two years doing odd jobs, sweeping up, running errands, living rough and eking out a living that was little better than back on his daddy's farm, Sanders met Miguel Fernandez, a Mexican bandit who'd seen enough of the future, and had enough of a brain, to organize his own little crime syndicate.

Fernandez was a smart cookie. He invested in both people and property and within two years, had set up a network that covered everything from prostitution, murder, protection and contraband. Doug Sanders saw this as the easy life, and it took him only a year to get himself established and well-favoured with Fernandez, who treated the boy like an adopted son.

He'd gone from strength to strength

eventually becoming Fernandez's right hand man, organizing everything and forever on the lookout for fresh scams.

Beef had been his brainchild and they now had a virtual monopoly on cattle that was raking in more money than even the prostitution racket.

But Sanders, unlike Fernandez, was not content to sit back behind a big desk and merely organize. He wanted to be in the thick of the action; maybe, he thought, because of his birthright as a farmer's son, he needed to get out of the city at times and get involved.

Sanders sat drinking whiskey he'd brought with him, none of the cheap rot-gut for him. He'd appeased the barkeep by donating half a dozen bottles for his personal use, so had little trouble taking over a small corner of the saloon for his own use and getting the sort of care and attention he'd been used to in the city.

So far his plans had gone like clockwork, with the exception of the young blond cowboy who'd threatened to expose him. That had troubled Sanders, not because he was bothered about being exposed, but because he'd hand-picked his team, and his judgement had been wrong. He'd always prided himself on being a good judge of character, and this minor flaw troubled him. He hoped he hadn't made the same mistake with the two gunmen he'd just hired in the bunkhouse.

★ ★ ★

Tom Hilks settled Aggie in with Harold and Sadie Meeks. Harold was busy in his store, but Sadie was certain he wouldn't object to having Aggie stay with them for a few days — in fact, she thought, he'd probably like Aggie to stay a lot longer. However, she put these thoughts to the back of her mind, for now, and helped Aggie unpack her scant possessions in the spare room.

"You're kinda sweet on Tom, aren't you Aggie?" Sadie asked.

"Sometimes," Aggie answered defensively; she knew what the female grapevine was like in Woebegone and didn't want any rumours circulating about her — there were enough of those already.

She knew that most of the men in town kept a light shining for her and that most of the women, although they never said anything to her, were jealous of her.

"Could do a lot worse than Tom," Sadie continued as she shook the eiderdown on the large double bed to air it. It had been a long time since anyone had slept over at the Meeks's place.

"Yes, I suppose. I just don't know whether I'm ready to get involved. Besides, there's plenty of time for marriage."

Sadie stopped plumping up the bolster and carefully thought of her next sentence. What she wanted to say was: you haven't got that much time for marriage and children, you're thirty, high time you settled down. What she actually said was: "Well, it'd be nice to have a baby while you're still young enough to enjoy it."

Aggie knew *exactly* what she meant.

Sadie finished airing the bed and plumping the bolster while Aggie hung the few clothes she'd brought with her in the heavy oak wardrobe that Sadie had spent a fortune on obtaining from San Francisco.

"Let's have some coffee," Sadie suggested, and the two women walked through to the kitchen, where they'd left Tom.

"Settled in?" he asked.

"Yes, thank you," Aggie replied.

"Mighty fine of you to take her in, Sadie," Tom said.

"My pleasure, Tom. Anything to help *you two*," Sadie said and her emphasis was as clear as daylight.

"Well, I'll leave you two ladies to get on," Tom said rising from his chair. "Got me some checking up to do."

"Will we see you later, Tom?" Sadie

asked. "Maybe you'd like to come by for supper?"

"Thank you. I'd love to," Tom said.

"Let's say seven, then?"

"Seven it is," Tom said, tipped his hat and left.

Aggie just looked at Sadie. She knew what the woman was up to. Matchmaking was so damn obvious, her motives were just as transparent. It seemed every married woman in Woebegone wanted to get Aggie married off to take temptation away from their own husbands.

Aggie sighed, and sipped at the boiling hot coffee. It was going to be a long day, she thought.

★ ★ ★

Harold Meeks was busy doing nothing in his store. He knew he'd have few, if any, customers while that damn catalogue wagon was in town. The herd was due to transfer on tomorrow and it would take two, maybe three weeks for things to get back to normal. He knew that what sales he had lost he'd never recover, but he'd make damn sure that his prices went up a tad, not enough for folks to moan about, but enough to make a point.

He spent his time checking over his stock, making a list of things he'd better order. Maybe he'd have a word with that Sanders fellow and see what's left on the covered catalogue wagon. Maybe he'd want to get rid of any stock he had left on his hands at a cheap price. A very cheap price, Meeks smiled to himself. He might have the last laugh yet.

Still, he thought, the drovers would need some last minute stuff, usually tobacco, hard tack, jerky, that sort of thing. Maybe even some candy to chew on the trail. He'd make some sales before the herd got going again, then it would be another three months before the next herd hit town.

Filling up the glass jars along the

front of the counter, Harold made sure that the candy was well in eyesight, next to the tobacco. They might not think about candy, but if it was stuck under their noses, he knew they'd buy it.

The glass-fronted cabinet on the wall behind the counter was cram-filled with ammunition. Another good seller, he thought as he turned to survey its contents. Every box with the label the right way round, easy to see, easy to read — for them that could.

Satisfied that all was as well as it could be, Harold sat behind his counter and began to read the *Los Angeles Herald* he'd been saving. Although it was a month or so out of date, he enjoyed the reading.

★ ★ ★

Tom made his way over to the livery stable, where there was a makeshift mortuary. Woebegone wasn't big enough for an undertaker as such — they didn't even have a doctor — but Crooked Grin took care of most ailments and he also buried the dead.

The young cowboy was lying under a canvas in the corner of the livery stable, Tom knew he'd be burying him soon, there was always the risk of disease and flies and other insects only needed a few hours before they started in on a body. Besides, it wasn't good for the horses or the cattle out back. They could smell death.

"Howdy," Tom said as Crooked Grin approached, pitch-fork in hand.

"Tom. You found out who he is?"

"No. I'll have a word with the trail boss, see what he knows, but the two fellas who killed him split up on the trail. Weren't no sense in me runnin' off on a wild-goosechase."

"We found nothing on the body," Crooked Grin said, knowing that Tom would ask the question. "It okay if bury him now? Horses start to get jittery."

"Yeah, sure. You carry on. I'll tell Harold, as he's actin' mayor. He'll sort out the finances."

Crooked Grin nodded and tied the end of the sacking together. Town funerals got no coffin. He lifted the body onto his shoulder and dumped it unceremoniously on the back of a buckboard and, grabbing a shovel, set off for what was laughingly called Boot Hill. Laughingly, because it wasn't a hill, it was the shallow end of a valley on the outskirts of town.

Tom watched as the wagon set off down the street, then headed across to the saloon in search of Doug Sanders.

He found the man surrounded by his lackeys sitting inside the saloon in the far corner.

"Mr Sanders?" Tom asked, knowing who the man was.

"Sheriff."

"Seems like maybe one of your boys has been gunned down." Tom said, keeping both conversation and tone light.

Sanders leaned back in his chair and pulled a cigar from his inside

52

pocket and bit the end off, spitting it disdainfully to the sawdust-covered floor.

"Ain't had a report o' no shootin'," Sanders said, lighting up the cigar.

"Well, I ain't sure if he's one of yours or not," Hilks said. "But he ain't a local, an' I don't recall seein' him round town."

"What he look like," Sanders asked.

"Youngish, maybe mid-twenties, blond hair. Didn't have no identification on him."

"Sounds like Billy-Ray to me, what you think boys," Sanders grinned and eye-balled his cronies. They laughed, nodding agreement.

"Yeah, sure sounds like Billy-Ray," Sanders said and picked up a whiskey tumbler, draining its contents. Then added: "Any funeral expenses, I'll be glad to meet 'em."

"Kind of you, Mr Sanders. See Crooked Grin over to the livery stable. He's just buried him."

Tom Hilks tipped his hat and left

the saloon. There was something he didn't like about Sanders. He mentally shrugged his shoulders, thinking some folks you like, some you don't.

★ ★ ★

Jasper Dent and Wild Man Bore were well out of it. They'd drained their whiskey bottles and both men had collapsed on the bunks, their snores loud enough to wake the dead.

It was Dent who came to first, his head pounding like a herd of wild buffalo. He reached across and shook Bore, noticing the thin trail of spittle that ran from the sleeping man's mouth, down his chin and had dripped onto the filth of his shirt.

"We gotta get some clothes," he said more to himself than Bore.

Bore grunted, then continued snoring.

Dent got to his feet, swayed, then fell back down again. "Maybe I'll try later," he said out loud and closed his eyes.

After a few moments he opened them again to see the interior of the bunkhouse swirling around like a whirlygig. Dent sat bolt upright, then threw up over Bore.

Still the other man slept.

4

TOM HILKS made his way back to the Meeks's house, he figured Aggie would be settled in by now and maybe a bit more relaxed. He needed — but doubted he'd get — a more detailed description from her, otherwise it was like looking for a needle in a haystack.

Sadie Meeks and Aggie were seated in the kitchen as he knocked on their back door. He didn't want to use the front, too many loose tongues in Woebegone that always made something out of nothing.

Sadie opened the door and Tom caught the aroma of freshly brewed coffee that set his mouth to watering. He could never have too much coffee.

"Tom," Aggie said, her eyes regaining a little of their old sparkle.

"You feel like talkin' some more?" he asked her.

"Not much more to tell, Tom," she said. "I hadn't seen the two men around town before. Probably drifters, long gone by now."

"Maybe," Tom said, but he didn't sound convincing and he didn't know why.

"I'd like, if you don't mind Sadie, for you to stay here another couple of days, just 'til I get this thing sorted out, one way or another." Tom sat at the large kitchen table and Sadie placed a mug of coffee in front of him.

"Stay as long as you like, Aggie," Sadie said. "Nice to have some company while Harold's at the store."

"Thanks, Sadie. Maybe a day or two," Aggie said.

Tom Hilks drained his coffee mug, even though it was scalding hot. "Well, if there's nothin' more you recall, I guess I'll take a walk round town, see what gives."

"If I do recall anything, Tom," Aggie

said. "You'll be the first to know." Aggie stood and smiled at Tom. She felt like putting her arms round him and giving him a kiss. But not in front of Sadie.

Tom, feeling slightly awkward, smiled back, twiddling with the brim of his hat as he stood there, embarrassment etched along his weather-beaten features.

Sadie stood and took it all in. She saw what was going on between the two and, although her lips didn't show it, she smiled.

* * *

The atmosphere in the bunkhouse was stifling. The sacking across the windows were drawn tight shut and the smell of the two stinking bodies of the only remaining inhabitants — mixed with the vomit — was almost overpowering.

Jasper Dent opened one eye and stared at the gloom-filled room. His eye stared at the ceiling — soot-blackened timber beams — that seemed alive with flies.

He opened his other eye and tried to sit up. The throbbing in his head stopped that little manoeuvre. He rested his head back on the soiled pillow and closed his eyes again, breathing heavily.

Keeping his eyes shut, he raised himself on to one elbow and slowly attained a sitting position. There he waited a few minutes, the throbbing in his head slowly subsiding. But then he heard the noise.

From another bunk, Bore's open mouth was making a noise like a herd of buffalo in rutting season. The sound suddenly filled Dent's head and he covered his ears with both hands, standing, shakily, at the same time.

He walked across to the near-comatose figure of his old partner and kicked a leg of the bunk. Bore grunted, snorted, but didn't wake up.

Dent staggered across to a rough-hewn wooden shelf where a cracked bowl, half full of murky, tepid water stood. He splashed his face. It didn't make him feel any better, so he did it again with the same result.

Then he picked up the bowl and emptied its contents over Bore's face.

Mouth open, Bore sucked in a lungful of water and almost choked.

"What the hell! Who did . . . what the hell!" he spluttered, spitting up water which dribbled down the filth of his shirt.

"You was snorin' fit to wake the dead," Dent said as he sat again on the edge of his bunk.

Bore stood. "Gotta take a piss," he said, and walked to the rear of the bunkhouse, tugging at his fly-button.

He stood facing a wooden wall and grunted as his bladder emptied, sending a pool of water that collected on the floor.

"We gotta eat," Dent said. "I got a hangover fit to die from. I've a good mind to shoot that lousy barkeep. I don't know what they made that rot-gut out of, but it weren't whiskey!"

Bore sat with his head in his hands, the stench of the vomit hit his nose but he hardly noticed. Dent did.

"This place stinks. I gotta get out o' here."

He pulled back the sacking from one window and the sunlight pierced his eyeballs like a Bowie knife. He tugged them shut again.

Bracing himself, he tentatively opened the sacking once more, acclimatizing his eyes to the brilliant sunlight that managed to make its way in through the dirt-engrained windows.

Blinking rapidly, trying to get the ache from his head to subside, Dent stared straight ahead into the main street of Woebegone. He stopped blinking and his lips parted in a leer. There, walking down the street was Aggie Miller.

"Come on, boy," Dent said, hitching up his trousers and spitting on both hands before rubbing them together in some vain hope of cleaning them.

"What the hell," Bore stammered.

"That li'le woman is out there as bold as brass," Dent said.

"What li'le woman?"

"You stupid sonovabitch! *That* li'le woman." Dent grabbed Bore by the scruff of his neck and pulled him over to the window.

Bore spat at the warped pane of glass and rubbed it with his fingers. The trail dust on the inside of the window turned to a brownish soup, obliterating the view almost entirely.

"Goddamnit!" Dent said. He grabbed hold of the sacking and rubbed the mess away.

"Look. There."

"She sure is a purty lump o' flesh," Bore said, the lascivious look on his face enough to worry a polecat.

"She's maybe gotta come back this way," Dent said. "Why don't we invite her in a-whiles?"

Bore laughed. "Seems like a neighbourly thing to do," he said. "Mighty neighbourly."

Bore almost fell to the ground in

a fit of laughter that turned into a coughing attack that took his breath away.

Dent spat on the floor, closely followed by Bore. Then both men resumed their watch of the lovely Aggie Miller as she walked downtown with Sadie Meeks.

★ ★ ★

Doug Sanders was out at the corral, speaking to his foreman. Well, he wasn't his foreman, he was the man who'd ramrodded the cows this far and Doug was trying to persuade him to stay on and head on out to Los Angeles with promises of more money and a better life.

Hank Bryan was a lean, tall cowboy who'd spent his thirty-seven short years in the saddle. Leaving home at fourteen to seek fame and fortune, he'd bedded down on his first night out on private property. He'd no sooner got to sleep than he was dragged through the dirt to a house bigger than he'd ever seen in his life.

There, after a short burst of interrogation — seemed like there'd been too much rustling going on for the owner's liking — he was hired.

Starting out looking after calves whose mothers died giving them life, he bottle-fed and weaned, brushed down and watered almost anything on four legs. As he grew older and stronger, he was on fencing duty, building and repairing, before he started bronco busting and finally, cattle driving — the love of his life.

He'd prided himself on maintaining a tight camp; hiring men he could trust and not losing any cattle without a fight — whether through disease, lack of water or Indian attacks and rustlers.

There was something about Sanders that didn't quite ring true and Hank turned the man down flat, saying he had to get back to the ranch but that there were more than enough men available to see the herd through.

Now, if there was one thing Sanders didn't like, it was a refusal — on whatever grounds. Billy-Ray had found that out and it had cost him his life.

Sanders smiled at the man, turned on his heels and, without uttering another word, he walked away.

If Hank Bryan could have seen Sanders' face he might have taken more care over his personal safety.

It took Sanders five minutes to organize one of his henchmen to maybe 'accidentally' bump into Hank Bryan. Ten minutes later, as Hank headed over to the saloon for beer, he was confronted by a man he'd never seen before in his life.

At first it had seemed like an innocuous meeting; the stranger walked out of the general store and straight into Hank, sending him sprawling in the dirt.

Brushing himself off, Hank stood and looked at the man, sort of expecting an apology, or some sign of regret. What he got was a steely-eyed stare.

"You could at least 'pologize, mister," Hank said as grabbed his Stetson from the street.

"Fer what?" the man said between teeth clenched around an unlit cigar stub.

"Fer what? Hell, for knocking me over, that's fer what."

"Seems like you walked into me, mister," the man said, widening his stance as he did so.

Hank looked at the man. Even though the sun was blazing down, he wore a range-coat that reached to the top of his boots. He was clean shaven and the canvas coat was clean.

"Hell, I ain't arguin'," Hank said and began to walk away.

"Seems like you are, mister," the man said.

"No, I ain't," Hank said pointedly.

"You callin' me a liar?"

Hank Bryan stopped dead in his tracks. He was standing in the middle of the street with his back to the stranger and felt more vulnerable than he ever had before in his life.

"No," he said eventually. "I ain't callin' you nothin'."

"Say what?"

"I said," Hank turned and faced the man, noticing his range-coat open and pulled back over the handle of a sideiron, "I ain't callin' you nothin'."

The man stepped down off the boardwalk and faced Hank, legs apart, right arm hanging loosely and easily by the wooden-handled gun.

"I don't take kindly to bein' called 'nothin'," the man said and spat the cigar into the dust. Hank watched it as it landed, sending a fine spray into the air that the wind caught and whisked away.

In that instant, Hank Bryan knew the man meant to draw. He knew there was no way of altering the situation he was in, no matter what he said or did.

"I ain't got no argument with you, mister," he said.

"Yeah, well I sure have with you. Make your play," the stranger demanded, flexing the fingers on his right hand and digging both heels into the dirt.

Hank's brain raced. He was no gunman, and he could tell by the other man's posture that he was.

"I said make your play, mister. 'Less you're yeller, o' course."

A silence descended on Woebegone. It appeared that everyone in the vicinity was well aware of what was about to take place.

From the saloon on the opposite side of the street, Doug Sanders struck a match and lit a cigarette as he peered, seemingly half-interested in the scene outside.

Hank was all too aware of the heavy silence that surrounded him. A stranger himself, with most of his hands still taking care of the herd, he knew he'd find no help.

Hank decided to swallow his pride. "Look, mister, I ain't no gunman. I'm a trail-boss, pure an' simple. If'n I offended you, then I'm rightly sorry."

"I'm-a tellin' you for the third time, mister. Make your play."

Hank resigned himself to a showdown, he could see no escape. Even if he walked, he felt sure the man would backshoot him, rather than let him get away. A thousand thoughts filtered through his head, but one stopped and lingered; the conversation he'd had with Sanders.

Realization suddenly hit him. For the last thirty seconds of Hank Bryan's life, he knew what Doug Sanders was about to do.

Hank went for his gun, the barrel of his Colt exploded when it was still pointing downwards and he saw the crater the slug made in the dirt by his feet. He watched as the wind blew the sand across the hole and, in the blink of an eye, the crater was no more.

As soon as Hank went for his gun and as soon as the stranger was sure he'd drawn it, the tall man drew his own weapon. Using his left hand to cock the hammer, he drew, fired cocked and fired in one well-practised movement that took the minimum of effort.

As soon as the .45 left the barrel of his gun, Hank knew where it was headed and, although his brain yelled at him to move — duck, side-step, run away, anything — he stood and watched as the bullet slammed into his chest.

The involuntary twitching in his right hand squeezed the trigger of his own weapon and he was flung backwards — already dead as the lead pierced his heart — landing heavily in the centre of the street.

The heavy, cloying silence prevailed; now it seemed worse after the double explosion of the gunplay. The stranger walked across to the body of the man he'd just shot, his weapon still drawn and cocked again — just in case.

Hanks sightless eyes stared up into the brilliant blue of the afternoon sky, a sky he'd never see again.

Voices made the man turn, Colt in

hand. The town had come out of its hidey-hole to peek and nose around and see what all the fuss was about.

The tall man replaced his weapon and took out a fresh cigar, bit the end off and spat it into the dirt, struck a match on his gunbelt and inhaled deeply.

The small knot of people around Hank Bryan's body turned to stare at the man and then back at Hank.

From his office, Tom Hilks sighed as the shots went off. He stood up, put his gunbelt on and strode down the street to see what the hell was goin' on now.

He didn't have long to find out.

5

THE tall stranger was still standing over the dead body of Hank Bryan as Tom walked down the street, a small group of townsfolk had gathered but, as none of them knew either the living or the dead man, interest was minimal.

"You do this, mister?" Tom asked, almost unnecessarily.

"Sure did, Sheriff," the tall man replied and there was a hint of contempt in his voice.

"Man drew first, had no choice," he continued as he reloaded his weapon.

Tom knelt down by the side of the body and felt for a pulse. There was, of course, none to be felt.

Standing, Tom called out: "Any you folks see anythin'?"

There were a few murmurs before one man spoke up.

72

"Seen it all, Sheriff. Dead man drew first. No doubt 'bout it."

"What's your name, stranger?" Tom asked.

"Locklin," the man replied. "Chance Locklin. Some folks call me Last Chance Locklin," he grinned, showing even white teeth, but his eyes didn't reflect the grin.

"Plan on stayin' in Woebegone?"

"Hell no. Nothin' to do here. I'm with the drive. Work for Mr Sanders."

Sanders again, Tom thought. "You know who this man was?" Tom asked.

"Nope. Never seen him afore," Chance said. "That all, Sheriff?"

"I don't want you in town after sundown," Tom said. "Make sure you're well out of my sight."

"Anythin' you say — Sheriff," Chance spat out the last word and Tom didn't miss it.

"Someone get Crooked Grin," Tom yelled at no one in particular, but there was no need. Crooked Grin appeared on the scene, complete with sacking to cart the body away.

"Go through his pockets," Tom said. "I'll be over shortly."

Crooked Grin nodded, wrapped the sacking round the dead man and lifted the body onto his shoulders as if it were a bale of hay.

Tom set off to have a word with Doug Sanders.

★ ★ ★

Harold Meeks was in the middle of stocktaking as his wife and Aggie entered the store.

Still complaining bitterly about the catalogue-wagon Sanders had brought into town with the drive, he nevertheless wanted to be up-to-date as soon as the drive left and folks started shopping with him again.

"You still fussin' over your stock," Sadie said with a slight grin on her face.

"Fussin'? What you mean, fussin'? This here's an important part o'tradin',"

Harold said indignantly.

"Seems to me all you do is count things up," Sadie added.

"That's what stocktakin's all about," Harold replied. "An' it would sure take less time if'n I had some help 'stead o' hindrance!"

"You stay, Sadie," Aggie said. "I'll take a walk round town for a while. Could do with some air."

"You sure, honey?" Sadie asked.

"Positive."

"Well, if you're sure you'll be all right."

"You help Harold. I'll come back in say, an hour?" Aggie said.

"Hour'll be fine," Harold said.

"Let's hope I don't have to count every single jelly bean," Sadie said, removing her bonnet.

"Very funny," Harold licked his pencil and did some more figuring.

Aggie left the store. Despite their banter, she knew that Harold and Sadie were inseparable. They were both still complaining as she closed the door and stepped out onto the boardwalk.

The sound of the shots brought Aggie back to the real world. Automatically, she ducked down behind a trough. She was experienced enough to know that if some drunk cowboy was just shooting off his gun, stray bullets had a habit of hitting someone.

After the explosion of the two shots Aggie stayed where she was for a few moments, her breath coming in short gasps as she tried to calm herself down. The incident at her shack had had more effect on her than she thought.

Harold and Sadie came out of the store, a look of fear crossed their faces until they saw that Aggie was all right.

"I'm okay," Aggie said. "The shots came from the other end of town. Just a bit nervous, I guess."

"You get yourself back to the house," Harold said. "It ain't safe outside."

"Or come back to the store," Sadie pleaded.

"I'm all right. Honest," Aggie said.

"I'll walk back to the house if it makes you happy."

"It'd make me more'n happy if you stayed there," Sadie said.

"I will. Now you two get on." Aggie smiled and watched as Harold and Sadie went back inside the store.

Aggie continued her stroll. The town was quiet and she wasn't curious enough to find out what the shooting was all about. She figured it best not to know.

Restless — the events of earlier that day gradually receding from the front of her mind — Aggie wandered to the far end of town, looking down the trail towards her shack, which was at least two miles further on.

Thoughts of her long-disappeared husband came flooding back and in her mind's eye, his face drifted in and out of focus until it was hard to distinguish between him and Tom Hilks.

She smiled as she thought of Tom. The only other man she'd slept with and the guilt had been pretty strong, that's why, she told herself, she hadn't slept with him again — yet. She knew she would though, it was just a matter of time.

Old Charlie was just coming out of the sheriff's office, bucket and mop in hand, he threw the contents of the bucket into the dirt and spat after it and, without looking up, he waddled back down the street to who knew where.

Just where *does* old Charlie live? she thought to herself, and then dismissed the thought. Not that she didn't care, it just wasn't any of her business. Old Charlie did well enough, and he seemed perfectly content.

At the far end of town, Aggie stopped and gazed out into the desert. The reflected sunlight burned into her eyes as she stared at the almost perfect yellowness of the sand, broken up here and there with cactus seeming to stand sentinel. A few parched trees, she counted five, and the odd ball of sage blowing free in the breeze.

The land shimmered in the heat of the afternoon and as she watched, water formed and disappeared again before her very eyes. A huge lake of clear blue, crystal cool water. There and gone in an instant.

She turned on her heels and began to walk back towards the Meeks's house, just a hundred yards down the dusty street. Level with the bunkhouse, she saw the drapes move. They opened and closed swiftly, and she thought nothing of it.

She thought nothing of it right up until the hand closed around her mouth, while another arm went round her waist and began dragging her backwards.

The parasol she was carrying dropped into the dirt and she disappeared into the bunkhouse.

★ ★ ★

Tom Hilks stood over the body of the man he now knew to be Hank Bryan.

The man looked to be in his late twenties, maybe early thirties. Tom knew he'd come in with the herd. Whether he worked for the purchaser or the buyer, he'd yet to find out.

He'd assumed Doug Sanders would still be in the saloon, but the place was practically deserted.

"Nothin' else on him, Crook?" Tom asked Crooked Grin.

"Only few dollars. Nothing else," Crooked Grin replied and handed over a ten and six ones.

"You may as well keep that, expenses," Tom said. "That'll save the town payin' fer the funeral."

"I bury him now?" Crooked Grin asked.

"Might just as well, don't think there'll be any mourners," Tom said.

Crooked Grin grabbed his shovel, threw the body onto his buckboard and, without another word, set off for Boot Hill for the second time that day. Inwardly, he was cursing his luck. If only he'd waited a bit longer, he would have only had to dig one hole.

Tom walked round to the rear of the livery stable. The noise that the steers generated was deafening once you got out into the huge corral. Surrounded on three sides by buildings, the town was protected from both noise and smell as the prevailing breeze took most out into the desert.

There were a few cowboys working amongst the herd. Some cows had given birth and had to be separated from the main herd and the calves branded so they didn't get mysteriously lost.

Tom approached the nearest cowboy. He described the dead man and showed him his wallet.

"Hell, yes. Sure I know him. He was the trail boss," the man said. "Where is he now?"

Tom explained that Crooked Grin had taken the body out to Boot Hill.

"'Cuse me, Sheriff," the man said. "But Hank was a mighty popular trail boss. I think the rest o' the men should know about this."

"You want me to hold the funeral up?" Tom asked.

"'Preciate it if'n you could, Sheriff."

The man looked genuinely upset, he'd obviously lost a friend. He thought for a while before asking the obvious question.

"How'd he die?"

"Gunfight," Tom said.

"Fair?"

"So far as I can tell."

"You know who was responsible?"

"Yeah. A stranger. Locklin, Chance Locklin."

"Locklin? Sanders man?"

"You know him?" Tom asked.

"I know *of* him," the man replied. "I sure do know of him."

"Like to fill me in?" Tom said.

"Locklin is a bully boy. Sanders uses him to get his own way. He's bin tryin' to get us to stay on to drive the herd to Los Angeles, but me an' most o' the boys don't trust him. We've heard tell Sanders is the biggest crook there is, in cahoots with some Mex.

"So we figure our job's over. We're just waiting on our pay now which is over to the bank yonder."

Tom chewed this information over. It would take at least two weeks to check up on Sanders and by that time he'd be well gone.

"I'll catch Crooked Grin up and then meet you back here, say in an hour. Okay?"

"Sure. I'll get the boys together. Them that's here, anyways."

Tom hightailed it out of town; he'd knew he'd have no trouble catching up with the buggy, so he didn't punish his horse any.

★ ★ ★

"She sure is a peach, an' that's no lie," Bore said as he placed Aggie on one of the filthy bunks. He raised his fist and smashed it into her jaw. He didn't use all his strength, he knew he didn't have to. The last thing Aggie saw was the huge knuckles as they swept through the air towards her. The peaceful oblivion.

"I'm-a gonna enjoy this," Dent said, even though his head was still throbbing with the effects of the cheap whiskey.

"Better tie an' gag her," Bore said. "Ain't likely we'll be disturbed, but if she starts a-yellin' . . . " He left the sentence unfinished.

Dent removed his bandanna, sticky with his sweat, and forced it across Aggie's mouth. Bore tied her hands behind her back, then her feet, legs splayed wide, to the foot of the bunk.

Bore could not stop himself grabbing Aggie's breasts through her dress and he squeezed them hard.

"Don't damage the goods," Dent said and both men laughed.

They stopped abruptly when they heard horses outside the bunkhouse.

"Quick," Dent said, "help me cover her up."

They piled blankets and sheets and a saddle on the bunk. Now, even if she came to, no one would know she was there.

Two men walked into the bunkhouse: "Mr Sanders wants to see you. Now," they commanded and waited for the two men to follow them.

Reluctantly, Dent and Bore left the bunkhouse, leaving Aggie unconscious on the bunk. Still, they both thought, there was always later.

6

EVENING drew close. The sun's rays began to flicker in the heat rising up from the arid ground around Woebegone. Anyone riding into town at this time of the day wouldn't have to guess how the town got its name.

The sun-bleached boards of the few permanent buildings, almost fried to a crisp, along with the boardwalk, gave the impression of being a ghost town. Tumbleweed ran through the only street, unhindered by man or animal, only to disappear out the other side of town.

Dent, Bore and Sanders' henchmen were the only sign of life as they rode out of town. The dust cloud kicked up by the four horses was choking as the lifeless air seemed to taste each grain of sand before letting it fall, lazily, back to the ground again.

The water trough outside the livery stable had a fine coating of dust that floated on top of the water, not heavy enough to sink, not big enough to soak the water up.

Inside the livery stable, Crooked Grin and Clem Watkins were getting ready to call it a day.

Crooked Grin had a coffin to build, but he couldn't start that until the animals had been fed and watered.

The body of Hank Bryan, still wrapped loosely in sacking, was beginning to bloat in the heat. The effect on Clem was minimal, but Crooked Grin was uneasy. Being Indian, tribal views and customs were strong in his head even though he couldn't ever remember living with his tribe, and leaving a dead man for too long without burial, even a paleface, bothered him.

Tom had ridden back in with the buckboard, after much persuasion on his part to get Crooked Grin to turn around. The fact that the dead man's friends wanted a decent, Christian, burial in the morning was of little concern to Crooked Grin. He was worried the man's spirit would be lost well before sun-up.

The promise of extra money didn't allay his fears either. If Crooked Grin had had his way, the dead man would have been burnt on a funeral pyre so that his spirit could rise with the smoke, but he knew these Christians didn't do things the proper way, not like real human beings: Indians.

The last stall had been cleaned out, the last horse fed and watered and even groomed.

"Reckon I'll check on the steers," Clem said.

"Me build coffin," Crooked Grin said and disappeared to get the wood.

Clem watched him go and then left the stable to check the pens.

Tom, meanwhile was busy drafting a letter to the chief of police in Los Angeles, requesting information on a certain Doug Sanders. He knew it'd take a minimum of ten days before he heard back — if he ever did — but he went through the motions.

All he had to do now was persuade a rider to take the letter, wait for a reply and bring it on back, by which time, Tom mused, Sanders would be well out of Woebegone.

★ ★ ★

The ride out to where Sanders had set up camp took only ten minutes. Neither Dent nor Bore had ever seen anything like it. Sanders's tent was like a palace. Inside there were four different areas, with an awning outside under which was set a table and six chairs complete with glasses, place settings and a candelabra with seven candles burning — and it wasn't even dark yet!

One of the rooms was a wash house — bathroom, Sanders called it — and it was into this room he showed the two men.

89

"Now if you'll be good enough to wash and brush up," he said, "there are some clean clothes; we'll burn the ones you're wearing."

Bore and Dent were too dumbstruck to say anything. Wash and brush up!

"Shit an' hell!" Bore said as he stripped off his filthy shirt revealing an even dirtier undervest.

"Cain't say I'm lookin' forwards to this," Dent said as he followed suit.

The two men stood in their longjohns and splashed water from the bowl onto their upper bodies. Within a matter of minutes, the water left in the bowl resembled a thick, brown soup.

To the side of the bowl were two cut-throat razors, two brushes and a bowl of shaving soap; hanging to the left of those was a leather strop that looked as if it had never been used.

"I ain't shavin', an' that's an end to it," Bore said, studying his face in the mirror that hung over the bowl. "I like ma beard an' I aim to keep it!"

"Don't go bellyachin' to me, pard,"

Dent said. "Think I'll have me a shave though. I got critters livin' in there eatin' better'n I do!"

There were two elegant gilt chairs either side of the tent flap that led into the bathroom and on each of these was a complete set of clothes — even down to boots.

Dent finished shaving and looked at his face in the mirror. The growth he'd removed took years off his life — at least in his eyes — and he felt pretty damn good.

"How's he know them clothes is gonna fit?" he said to Bore.

"Damned if I know. One ways to find out," Bore said and grabbed at the nearest pile.

The Levis were new, as were the shirt and longjohns and, although Bore grabbed the wrong pile as he quickly discovered, the clothes fitted both men as if they'd been measured up for them.

"I ain't wearing no cissy-socks," Bore spat.

"Don't think I's ever worn 'em," Dent said. "But I reckon I'll try 'em."

Dent sat on one of the chairs and put the socks on. "Hell, they feel good," he said.

"They'd've felt better if you'd washed your feet first."

Both men turned at the sound of the voice from behind them. Doug Sanders stood in the entranceway, a cigar burning between the fingers of his right hand and a fine glass delicately gripped in the other, containing red wine.

"Dinner is about to be served," Sanders said and waited while the two men donned their boots.

"How come you knew what size we was?" Bore asked.

"I make it my business to know everything," Sanders said in a way that Dent and Bore didn't doubt.

"How come you's treatin' us like we was somebodies?" Dent asked.

"I treat *all* my employees the same," Sanders said easily. "Unless, of course, they cross me. Things change then."

"Who said we was your *employees*?" Dent said stressing the last word, he wasn't sure quite what it meant.

"You took my money. That means you're hired," Sanders said and took a puff on his cigar, blowing out the uninhaled smoke into the bathroom.

"'Pend on what you hired us fer," Bore said, now fully clothed.

"That's what we have to discuss. But first, we eat. I've got to make up my mind yet as to whether or not you can be trusted with the job I have in mind."

Dent gave Bore a sideways glance: one thing the two men had in common was their unasked for and untalked about trust in each other. Now it was being questioned by a third party and Dent took exception to the remark.

"Mister, I ain't never done no job for nobody, an' I don't aim to start now." Dent slapped on his gunbelt and Sanders caught a glimpse of the Colt's handle.

"Pity," Sanders said. "I would've thought that two thousand dollars might have helped to change your mind."

"*Two thousand dollars?*" Dent stood with his mouth open in disbelief.

"Nothing wrong with your hearing, Mr Dent."

"What you want that pays that sorta money?" Dent asked.

"That, for the moment, is for me to know. In the meantime, I suggest we eat before the steak gets cold. This way — gentlemen." Sanders turned on his heel and left the tent. Dent and Bore followed.

For the first time the aroma of the cooking filled their nostrils and they both realized they were hungry enough to eat a steer each — right down to the tail!

★ ★ ★

Harold and Sadie had finished counting everything in the store — except the floorboards — and Harold even knew how many of them there were.

"Let's go eat," he said to his wife.

"Have you locked up out back?" she asked.

"Sure have. Can't be too careful when drovers're in town." Harold removed his apron and folded it up neatly, placing it on the glass-topped counter ready for business the following day — if there *was* any business, that was.

"Reckon the herd'll be leavin' tomorrow," he said absently to his wife. "People'll start comin' back to the store then."

"You fixed them prices up?" Sadie asked, knowing full well that he had.

"Five cents across the board," Harold said, smiling. "'Cept for the candy. I ain't put the price o' that up."

Sadie smiled at her husband. They didn't have any children of their own — even though they'd tried for years, nothing seemed to happen — and they were now at their time of life when maybe it was a mite too late. But Harold's love of the children in town, of which there were no more than a dozen at any one time, was obvious.

Sadie knew that for every candy bar he sold, another just went missing, and Sadie had a good idea where they went.

"Come on," she said, staring at her husband with a look on her face that was filled with love for the man she'd spent the past seventeen years looking after. "Let's go eat. Aggie will be wondering where we got to."

"Aggie! I plum forgot her," Harold said and grabbed his jacket, fishing in the pockets for the key to the store's front door.

"Fine way to treat a guest," he mumbled as he ushered his wife out and locked the door behind him.

"Aggie can look after herself," Sadie said, "which is more'n I can say for some folk."

"An' what's that meant to mean? You're talkin' 'bout me, ain't ye?"

"If the boot fits," Sadie said and smiled at her man as she slipped her arm through his.

The town was deserted. Pretty soon, they both knew, the drovers who'd been in town for three days now, would be coming in to the saloon. Tomorrow, they'd be paid in full for the drive and then most of them would go their separate ways, except the ones hired to see the herd through to Los Angeles.

"Hell!" Harold said. "I left that paper in the store."

"It'll keep," Sadie said. "Give you somethin' to do tomorrow."

Harold thought about that and he had to agree. Last day before the herd shipped out and the store would be dead. The drovers bought everything from that damned Sanders. He'd not seen hide nor hair of any of them.

He'd begun to think that maybe it was a sign of the times. The town wasn't really big enough to keep him in business and, in times of drought, and there were plenty of those, the folks roundabout didn't have the cash to pay for goods anyway.

That smart-alec bank manager had been foreclosing on three or four homesteads lately. Didn't even give the owners a chance to work their way out before kicking them out.

Yeah, Harold thought, maybe it's a sign of the times.

"You reckon we ought to maybe make a move?" he said to his wife.

"An' do what?" she asked. "Folks round here depend on the store in times of trouble."

"Trouble seems to be visitin' Woebegone too often for my likin'," Harold said. "'Sides, they ain't never gonna be able to clear off their debts an' I can't keep extendin' their credit."

"We all gotta do what we can, Harold," Sadie said. "We all gotta do what we can."

They climbed the four steps that led to the verandah of their small home. Harold opened up the front door and stood to one side to let Sadie enter first. Still got his manners, she thought as she went inside.

The drapes were still drawn. The sun, having a nasty habit of taking the colour out of everything, was Sadie's worst enemy and she fought it every day.

She opened up the drapes and let the last of the evening's light filter through the dust-covered windows. She used to clean them every day, but you only need one cart to pass by and they got covered again so now she cleaned them once a week, usually on a Sunday. Living in the middle of the desert, you had to compromise, she'd reasoned.

"Aggie? Aggie? We're back," Sadie called out, but there was no reply.

"Aggie?" Quickly, Sadie ran from room to room. There was no sign of Aggie.

"Harold, Aggie's not here!"

Harold looked out the back windows, hoping against hope that Aggie was in the swing-chair on the back porch, maybe taking a nap, but of course, she wasn't.

"I'll go see Tom," he said. "Maybe she's with him. Now don't you start to panicking nor nothin'. She'll be all right."

"You're right, Harold. I'm just a silly old woman," she said.

"No you ain't," Harold said. "You ain't old an' you ain't silly."

He gave his wife a quick hug.

"I'll be back afore you know it," he said and left the house. Unfortunately, he didn't feel as confident as he sounded.

Tom was still at his desk, the letter written, folded and ready in an envelope. He was pondering on who he'd get to ride to Los Angeles when Harold walked in.

"You seen Aggie?" he asked straight away.

"Harold. No, I thought she was with you."

Harold explained about the stock-taking and how Aggie said she was going back to the house.

"How long ago?" Tom asked.

"An hour, maybe two," Harold replied.

"Let's go," Tom said. An unseen hand had gripped hold of his guts and was squeezing a mite too hard. Despite his calm exterior, Tom felt that grip of fear.

Grabbing a rifle from the rack mounted on the wall, Tom and Harold left the office.

"Harold, could you check out the south side? I'll check the saloon and livery stable an' I'll meet you back here in say, fifteen minutes?"

"Sure thing, Tom," Harold said and set off at a trot, despite the heat.

Tom passed the old bunkhouse without a second glance. The sacking covering the windows was drawn tight and it never occured to him to check the place out.

★ ★ ★

Meal finished, both Dent and Bore were still waiting to find out what this 'job' was they'd been hired to undertake. But Doug Sanders was not a man to play all his cards in one go.

Piece by piece he'd listened as the two men had related some of their escapades in the past and he was now drawing up a picture of the characters of these two-bit crooks sitting round his fine dinner-table.

"You gonna tell us what you want doin'?" Dent asked.

"All in good time, gentlemen. All in good time. But for now, I suggest a nap is called for. If you'll excuse me."

Sanders stood and yawned exaggeratedly. "I suggest we meet again — here — at eleven o'clock."

"You mean we can go?" Bore said.

"For now, yes. But be here by eleven." Sanders left the table and entered his sleeping quarters.

A lascivious grin appeared on Bore's face. "This is our lucky day, pard," he said. "You a-thinkin' what I's a-thinkin'?"

Dent knew exactly what Bore meant. A full belly, some decent beer, clean clothes and that bitch back in the bunkhouse.

"I sure am, pard," Dent said. "But I go first."

"Reckon we'll toss a coin on that one," Bore said licking his lips and grinning from ear to ear.

"She sure is purty piece o' ass," he said. "An I am to take me a big slice o' that."

They all but ran to their horses in their eagerness to get back to the woman they'd left trussed like a turkey in the bunkhouse.

As they left the campsite Tom, more anxious than he'd ever been in his life, rode out to Aggie's place — just in case.

Harold had returned home and now had the task of comforting Sadie.

He'd told her they'd searched through the town to no avail and that Tom reckoned maybe she'd ridden on home to get some of her things, so he'd gone out there.

"Oh, Harold," Sadie said, a tear already forming at the corner of one eye. "I hope she has. I *really* hope she has."

Harold hugged his wife, all thoughts of eating had completely vanished as they both walked through to the kitchen to wait. It would turn out to be the longest night of their lives.

7

TOM reached Aggie's shack and, without waiting for his animal to come to a halt, he jumped to the ground and ran towards the front door. Colt in hand, he stopped and listened. There was no sound of movement, nothing. The still air seemed ominous and oppressive, silence hurting his ears as he concentrated all his attention.

The door was unlocked as he lifted the latch and the creaking of metal on metal as he slowly swung the door inwards assaulted his senses and was magnified beyond reality.

Inside, the shack was in darkness. The drapes, closed when Aggie had left, were still hanging across the three windows. Blackness filled his vision and, after the bright sunlight, his eyes took awhiles to become used to the murky interior.

Slowly, definition began to emerge. He picked out the overly-large table set in the centre of the small room, almost dwarfing everything. Chairs, a set of drawers, a vase of wild flowers and at the back of the living-room, the door that led to the kitchen and small bedroom.

It was obvious Aggie had not returned here, but Tom decided to check it out anyway — just to be on the safe side. He opened the door leading to the kitchen: neat, tidy, not a thing out of place. The bedroom — though really just a curtained off corner of the kitchen — was equally deserted.

Reholstering his gun, Tom stood and wondered where to look next. She couldn't have gone far. It was late in the day and Aggie was desert-wise enough to know not to wander off unprepared. She had to be in town. There seemed no alternative.

Closing the door behind him, Tom

set off back to town. Maybe there was somewhere I haven't looked yet, he thought as he tried to think positively, even though at the back of his mind and slowly creeping towards the front, the thought of Aggie in danger hung over him like a thick, black cloud.

★ ★ ★

Aggie had regained consciousness. The blackness she opened her eyes to was frightening beyond belief. The thick blankets and sacking that covered her body were impenetrable. Her hands and feet tied tightly and a gag over her mouth, hampered any attempt to get out from the covers.

It took a few minutes for her to remember the sequence of events leading to the quandary she now found herself in. Unwanted tears coursed down her cheeks as the memories flooded back. She gritted her teeth together — hard. She was determined to remain strong, even though she felt weak and helpless.

Twisting her wrists, she tried to loosen the bonds that restrained her. The rope was coarse and she felt it breaking the skin of her arms and then that warm, sticky feeling only blood can convey. No matter how hard she tried, the ropes remained tight, if anything, tighter.

The tears of alarm were now turning to tears of frustration and a sweat broke out on her forehead, adding to her discomfort.

Turning her head, she managed to dislodge a piece of sacking that covered her face. She inhaled deeply through her nose, the fetid air of the sacking now gone, the air seemed fresher, cooler, and she had at least accomplished something.

She was able, now, to see her surroundings. She often walked past the bunkhouse, but had never been inside. The only time it was ever used was when drovers were in town, or maybe when ranch hands, too drunk to get back to their ranches, stayed over for the night. And, of course, old Charlie.

Charlie used the place all the time. Kept it reasonably tidy, made sure there was enough wood for the burner and brushed up — occasionally.

Aggie hoped against hope that Charlie would be the next visitor; if he was, maybe she would survive, if not —

She closed her mind and concentrated on her predicament. She became aware, almost abstractedly, that she had no feeling in her feet and very little in her hands. Obviously, she thought, the blood supply was being cut to a minimum. Frantically, she began to move her fingers and toes in an attempt to get some feeling back. Slowly, a tingling sensation swept through her extremities — pins and needles — the pain was excruciating, but at the same time, relief flooded through her body, at least her feet and hands were still there!

Gingerly, she kept moving her fingers

and toes, helping the blood to circulate and ease away the pain of pins and needles.

The door opened and a shaft of light cut through the darkness like a knife, blinding Aggie temporarily. From the far end of the bunkhouse she heard shuffling feet and the sound of a broom being swept across the dirt-caked floorboards.

Charlie!

Aggie moaned as loud as she could, but the broom kept swishing, joined now by Charlie humming some tuneless song.

Aggie groaned and tried to kick the covers off her body, but the mound was too big and too heavy. Surely Charlie could both see and hear her?

Apparently not. Charlie was as deaf as a post and so short-sighted you had to be almost nose to nose before he recognized anybody.

The bunkhouse was filling with dust now as Charlie brushed, seemingly at random. He was not so much cleaning the floor as redistributing the dirt. He neither splashed water to damp the dust down, nor kept the door open, the result was a white fog that quickly filled the entire room.

Aggie turned her face to one side, breathing heavily through her nose as the dust began to settle everywhere. She even feared she'd choke to death before Charlie spotted her — if he ever did.

Mercifully, the door opened, but Aggie's gratitude to the breeze that helped clear the dust away was quickly tempered as she heard the voices.

"Well, hell! Looky what we got ourselves here." It was Dent and his cohort Bore back in town.

The broom continued to swish.

"Deaf to boot!" Bore said and laughed.

"Let's see how he feels," Dent said.

Aggie couldn't see what was going on, but the broom fell to the floor and a yell of pain filled the bunkhouse.

"Shit 'n' hell," Charlie gasped.

Dent had pricked Charlie's backside with his hunting knife and the old man was dancing round the floor like a two-year-old.

The cruel laughter of Dent and Bore filled Aggie's head.

"What the hell ya do that fer," Charlie spat out at the two men.

"'Cause we can," Dent said.

Now, old Charlie wasn't much of a gunman. Sure, he wore a sideiron, but nine times out of ten, he'd forgotten he had it, and on the odd times he'd drawn it, there had been no bullets in the chamber.

The gun, a Frontiersman, had seen, like Charlie, better days, and many folks in Woebegone were sure that if Charlie ever fired the gun it'd probably blow up in his hand.

The leather belt and holster were as time-scarred as the old man himself; the gun butt hanging loose where the holster had split many years ago.

Charlie went for his gun as the pain in his ass subsided a little.

Dent's knife slashed out and cut Charlie's throat before the old man had even managed to wrap his fingers round his gun.

A silence filled the room, broken only by grunts of laughter from Dent and Bore and then a gurgling sound that Aggie doubted she would ever get out of her head.

Charlie's hands went to his throat. A look of complete surprise filled his face. He moaned, once, but was unable to make any more sound as his life ebbed out of his neck.

The old man fell forwards onto his knees, blood pumping through his fingers. He collapsed, face first into the dirt that only moments ago he'd been brushing.

Aggie heard him fall. She couldn't see him, but she knew old Charlie was dead; she could smell his blood.

"Like cutting through a piece o' pie," Dent said as he knelt down and cleaned the blade on Charlie's shirt.

Charlie's body was lying in a pool of blood now that dripped through the floorboards and onto the ground beneath.

"We'd better dispose o' the body," Bore said.

"Dispose? Hell, yes. I like that word. 'Dispose'" Dent said, letting the word roll around his mouth like a lump of prime beef.

"Grab some sacking," Dent said, "and come dark, we'll dump him somewheres out in the desert."

Bore did as he was told without question or comment. Aggie began to wonder if they'd forgotten about her, but she didn't wonder for long. Silent tears for Charlie ran down her face and she wondered when her turn would come. For come it surely would.

★ ★ ★

As Charlie slipped into unconsciousness and finally death, Tom Hilks reined his mount to a halt outside his office. It was time, he felt, to organize a search party.

Frantic now with worry, Tom entered the jailhouse and grabbed spare slugs for both Winchester and Colt, before stepping back outside and heading off towards the corral at the rear of the livery stable.

He thought his best bet of getting some volunteers was with the drovers, as most of the men in town were a bit long in the tooth to go gallivanting through the desert.

There were seven or eight men on duty when Tom arrived, he walked up to the men he'd spoken to earlier that day.

"Need some help," Tom said and explained the situation.

"Hell, I can let you have four men, Sheriff. 'Fraid I need the rest to guard the steers," the man said.

"Four would be plenty," Tom said.

Within minutes, four men were saddled and, after giving them a description of Aggie — he noticed the men's eyebrows rise as he described her — the four rode off into the desert, two north two south.

Tom thanked the lead drover and set off to take a more careful look round town.

He checked the saloon again, but the bartender hadn't seen Aggie all day. He headed back to Harold and Sadie's place — just in case she'd returned.

Riding past the bunkhouse he thought about checking it over, Charlie would probably be in there. Dismounting he walked across to the door and tried to open it. The door was locked from the inside.

"Charlie! Charlie, you in there?"

There was no reply, but Tom didn't really expect to get one. If the old man was asleep inside, it'd take a herd of buffalo to wake him up and even then he wouldn't hear anyone calling him.

Tom walked round the side of the building and peered through the windows in turn, trying to see if there was any one in there, but the darkness inside and the sacking covering most of the windows made it impossible.

He banged on some of the windows and stuck his ear close to the clapboard; if he couldn't see Charlie, he reckoned, he should be able to hear the old man snoring.

He listened intently for a few minutes but he heard nothing. Tom decided to visit Harold and Sadie and then check out the bunkhouse when Charlie awoke.

* * *

Inside the bunkhouse, the fist that slammed into Aggie's face sent her back into unconsciousness two seconds after Tom called out Charlie's name.

Dent and Bore hid under the bunks as Tom Hilks circled the outside of the building; they even saw his face pressed against one of the panes on two occasions. The two men, lying side by side, grinned as they watched the sheriff.

Neither man said a word. Not because they were fearful of getting caught by the sheriff, they just didn't want him spoiling their fun.

After five minutes they heard a horse ride off and Dent slid across the floor to a window and watched as Tom Hilks rode down the street.

Pulling the cover off Aggie's body, Dent ripped at her dress. He tried to pull it all off, but with her arms tied behind her, he left it and grabbed at her undergarments, ripping those was easier and he stood over her semi-naked body, gazing in admiration at the breasts he'd just uncovered.

Bore joined him. "Hellfire, she sure is a mighty fine woman," Bore said, his voice quivering with lust. He leaned across and grabbed hold of one of her breasts, almost tentatively.

"Goddamn!" he said, "they sure feel good."

"Go get a buckboard," Dent said.

"Say what?"

"I figure if'n they's a-lookin' fer this

gal, then they'd've checked out her shack. What say you an' me head out thataways and have ourselves a night to remember?" Dent grinned at his pard.

Bore didn't need any further explanation.

"Hell yes!" he said and left to walk across town to the livery stable.

After he'd gone, Dent also felt Aggie's breasts then he covered her up and wrapped her in the blankets and sacking, loosely tying them so they wouldn't fall off, and waited for Bore to return.

Dent licked his lips and wiped the sweat from his brow. They had to meet Sanders at eleven, but both before that — and after — they were going to have the time of their lives.

8

HENRY WARTON, bored and fastidious, decided to do some paperwork in the bank that evening. It wasn't unusual. With no wife or family, Henry got bored very easily. The only thing that kept him sane was his paperwork.

With a single oil-lamp burning, Henry bypassed the time lock on the safe and retrieved his papers. With the drovers needing to be paid tomorrow, as well as the transfer of funds from Doug Sanders to herd owners, he thought he might as well make headway.

As was his custom when alone in the bank, he put a pot of fresh coffee on the wood-stove, tossed a couple of logs inside and sat at his desk.

He took out a cigar from his inside pocket and placed it on his desk — far corner, aligning with his pen-stand.

Placed a box of matches next to it, also aligned, and the heavy glass ashtray, which he kept in the right-hand bottom drawer, was placed centrally.

Satisfied that all was well, he removed the ink-pot lid and dipped his pen in the black ink. A smile, or what passed for a Henry Warton smile, passed his lips. All he was waiting for now was for the coffee to boil, then he'd light his cigar.

Outside, Wild Man Bore had hired a buckboard and was in the process of manoeuvring two nervous animals out of the livery stable. Crooked Grin watched as the man inexpertly drove the buckboard across the street and round the back of the bunkhouse.

Shaking his head, Crooked Grin looked up and down the street — deserted, as usual — and was about to re-enter the livery stable when the twinkling oil-lamp light from behind the shutters of the bank caught his eye.

Crooked Grin had seen the single

light many times before and he turned and went back inside to finish off the coffin.

Bore managed to halt the team more or less where it needed to be halted. He, too, had seen the light. Lashing the brake arm with the long leather reins, he jumped to the ground and had to stop himself from shouting out to Dent.

Running into the darkened bunkhouse, Bore, breathless, blurted out his news.

"Jasp, Jasp, there's someone over to the bank. I seen a light!"

"Calm down, could be anything," Dent replied, his mind more on Aggie.

"Don't you think we ought to check it out?" Bore went on.

Dent thought about that. Spat and nodded. "Yup, seems to me we might kill two birds with one stone here."

Bore looked confused.

"If'n the bank's got someone in it, mebbe we should change our plans," Dent went on. "Yeah! Mebbe, we should go rob it now, we'll load the woman in the back of the buckboard with the old man and then hightail it out to her place an' hole up a-whiles!" Dent's face creased in pleasure. Suddenly, everything was working out.

Dent checked on Aggie, she was still unconscious. He reached for her throat beneath the sacking and felt a good, strong pulse which satisfied him. For a moment, he thought he'd slugged her too hard and he didn't relish the thought of sleeping with a dead woman.

Lifting one end of the body, he told Bore to grab the other and, together, they carried Aggie out to the waiting buckboard.

"Grab some more o' that sackin'," Dent said, "I don't want no nosey parkers pokin' around."

Bore did as he was told and, when Jasper Dent was satisfied, he got Bore to move the buckboard down the alleyway and away from the bunkhouse to the rear of the bank building.

"Come on, let's go check this out," Dent said and, as Bore checked his handgun, Dent locked the door securely.

Night was almost upon them now. It didn't seem they'd only been in town a day — it felt like weeks. The warm breeze of the day had turned into a cold one now and they shivered, wishing they'd brought their range coats with them.

Ducking round the back of the bunkhouse, they made their way to the rear of the bank. Bore, gun in hand followed Dent's footsteps as though he was walking through a field of quicksand, unwilling to put a foot out of place.

Dent held his knife. One thing he didn't want was a lot of noise and the knife was as silent as the grave. The thought made him smile.

From the rear of the bank, through the only window, the watery glow of light just managed to seep from behind the blinds. There was only a small gap, through which Dent tried to peer, but he couldn't see anything.

The window itself was barred and locked, to try getting in this way would take all night.

Grabbing hold of Bore's arm, Dent led him away from the bank.

"I reckon we gotta go in through the front," he whispered hoarsely. "If whoever's in there only put the lock on, mebbe a boot will break it open."

Bore nodded, mainly because he couldn't think of a better plan.

"Now, as soon as I kick the door in, you make for the far left corner of the bank. If'n it's the manager in there, that's where he'll be," Dent said.

"S'posin' he's got a gun on him?" Bore said.

"Then you better be damn quick," Dent replied. "Now let's check out the street. We'll go separate ways, you take the left, I'll take the right. If'n you don't see any one, we'll meet at the front doors of the bank. Okay?"

"What if'n I sees someone?" Bore asked.

"Then we waits 'til theys gone. Clear?"

"Yup."

The two men split up and sidled round the side of the bank building, intending on meeting up at the front.

Dent got to the street first, he looked north and south, but the street was deserted; he made his way along the boardwalk. When he neared one of the front windows, the gap between frame and blind was wider and he was able to see inside the bank.

He couldn't believe his eyes. The safe was open!

Dragging his eyes off the safe, he saw Henry Warton sitting behind his desk. As he watched, Henry stood and walked across to the stove and, grabbing a cloth, picked up the coffee pot and poured himself a cupful, then returned to his desk.

Dent watched as Henry lit his beloved cigar, sending a plume of blue-grey smoke into the air.

Dent tore his eyes away from the window when he heard the heavy footfalls approaching. Bore! Idiot, he thought.

Dent drew a finger up to his lips and Bore acknowledged that he understood by tiptoeing along the boardwalk looking like the fool Dent knew him to be.

The two men reached the centre doors of the bank at the same time. Gently, Dent tried the handle — just in case the manager had forgotten to lock up. He hadn't, but the top of the door moved inwards slightly, telling Dent there were no bolts fastened on the inside.

The lock was centrally mounted and Dent took a step back, motioning Bore to stand to his left by the door — ready.

Bore grinned inanely, his Colt hanging loosely in his hand down by his side.

Jasper Dent lunged forward, his left leg raised, and his boot caught the door squarely. The door flew inwards and seconds later Bore raced through and towards the startled bank manager.

★ ★ ★

Harold and Sadie — feeling responsible — were beside themselves with worry when Tom arrived telling them there was no sign of Aggie.

"It's all my damn fault," Harold said, holding his head in his hands.

"Now, Harold, you can't blame yourself. Whatever has happened to Aggie would have happened anyways," Tom said, trying to calm the couple down.

"We'll find her," he continued. "It's just a matter of time."

"Forgive me, Tom," Sadie said, "where are my manners. Would you like a coffee?"

"Thanks, but no thanks. I can't rest up until I know Aggie is safe and well. I'll keep you posted. Now you two stay put — in case she returns. All right?"

The couple nodded and Tom left, intending to return to the bunkhouse and, come hell or high water, wake old Charlie up.

Leaving his horse tethered outside the Meeks' place, Tom walked down the street, passing the bank on his left and the livery stable on his right. He could hear the sound of hammering. Altering course, he entered the livery stable and saw Crooked Grin just about finishing off the coffin.

"Want a hand with the body?" Tom asked.

"Sure. Then I help search for Miss Aggie," Crooked Grin replied.

The two men lifted the body of Hank Bryan into the coffin and Crooked Grin nailed the lid on.

"Be glad when man is buried," the Indian said, "not good to be outside so long after death."

"Well," Tom said changing the subject, "I got two men north and two south circling round, trying to see if there's any trace of Aggie. I'm off to the bunkhouse. That's the only place I ain't searched so far. You seen Charlie around?"

"No."

"Well, I guess he's crashed out over there. You wanna come along?"

"I lock up first and see you there."

Tom left the livery stable, noticing the light on in the bank as he passed, but he was intent on getting old Charlie up and out so he could check out the place.

The bunkhouse was in darkness, the door still locked. Tom banged all hell on the door but got no response from inside. Taking out his sideiron, he pounded on the wooden walls until his arm ached. Still nothing.

Finally, frustration getting a firm grip, he returned to the door and kicked it down. Doubtless, the town council would have something to say about destroying town property, but the hell with them, Tom thought.

Feeling his way through the darkness, Tom made his way to the windows and began to systematically pull all the sacking to one side. Outside, the moon was taking over where the sun had left off, but the light wasn't strong enough to penetrate into the bunkhouse.

There had to be a lamp someplace, he thought. Stumbling into furniture and catching his shins on one of the bunks, Tom groped blindly until he found what he was looking for.

Striking a match, he lit the oil-lamp, waited until the wick was alight properly, lowered the glass dome and picked it up by the handle.

The sheriff had been in the bunkhouse many times before — usually to rouse sleeping cowboys who'd drunk too much the night before and weren't capable of getting home, so the state of the place came as no great surprise.

Filth was everywhere and Tom wondered what in the hell Charlie did in here. Nothing, by the looks of things.

Holding the oil lamp high to get maximum light, Tom scanned each bunk in turn: all were deserted, apart from rags that used to be blankets or sheets.

Dust and sand littered the floor, along with used bandannas and various articles of clothing that Tom didn't even want to guess about.

The lamplight caught hold of something that was out of place. Tom swung the lamp back and caught sight of a piece of cloth lying by the side of one of the bunks. Bending, he inspected it closer. Bright blue and clean, it hadn't been there long. With a start, he suddenly remembered the dress that Aggie wore: bright blue!

The door to the bunkhouse swung open and Tom went for his gun. Standing in the doorway was Crooked Grin.

"Jesus! You dang near scared me half to death," Tom said as he reholstered his Colt.

"Smell of blood!" said Crooked Grin.

"Say what?" Tom asked.

"Blood. There is blood in this place. Fresh." Crooked Grin began looking around the semi-dark room. He pointed to the floor near where the broom had been dropped.

"Here," Crooked Grin said flatly.

Tom brought the lamp across to where Crooked Grin, still pointing, was standing. The yellow light lit the floor and the dark red stain, although mainly soaked into the bone-dry floorboards, was only too obvious. Tom stood and stared, wondering how the hell he'd missed it in the first place.

Crooked Grin got down on his haunches and pushed a finger into the sticky mess. "Blood still wet. Someone died here tonight."

★ ★ ★

Henry Warton was more indignant than alarmed. He'd never been robbed in all his years of working in a bank, a mite unusual, but fact nonetheless.

"The bank is not open for business,"

he said calmly, replacing his cigar in the ashtray.

"Sure is now," Bore said and made his way across the empty room, gun pointing unwaveringly at Warton's head.

"Get to the safe," Dent said, following Bore towards Warton.

"This is an outrage!" Warton said, beginning to lose his cool.

"Outrage? That's a good word," Dent said. "An' that's what this is," he said and laughed.

"Now keep him covered," Dent said to Bore and he went to the double front doors of the bank and closed them shut, locking them from the inside with bolts top and bottom.

"There," he said finally, "now no one can surprise us."

Warton made a lunge towards the safe as Bore, still laughing from Dent's 'outrage' comment, had taken his eyes off the manager.

Warton managed to reach the safe door and threw all his weight at it in an attempt to close it. He failed. Bore stuck the barrel of his gun into the lock, and the door hit it hard, but didn't close.

In an instant, Dent was on Warton, knocking the man to the ground and pinning him there, his knife at the manager's throat.

"Now that was a plain dumb thing to do," Dent said calmly. "You could'a got yourself killed."

Warton stared up into the man's face, he looked him straight in the eye and for the first — and last — time, Henry Warton saw a madness there. A madness that was his own death.

Casually, Dent looked at Bore: "That safe still open?"

"Sure is," Bore said retrieving his gun. "Hell fire! He's dang broke ma gun!"

"That wasn't a clever thing to do, Mr Bank Manager," Dent said, turning his attention back to Warton. "I reckon you owe my pard, here, an apology."

Warton said nothing.

"Seems like he ain't gonna 'pologize, Bore," Dent said and in one swift movement, he brought his knife into play.

The sharp blade slit into the bank manager's neck like it was made of soft lard. At first, a thin red trickle of blood appeared and gently spread, catching Warton's white collar.

Quickly, the thin trickle turned into a deluge of blood. Dent stood up, the spray coming from the dying man's wound was all over him.

"Watch him dance," Bore said as they both looked at the gurgling, bloody mess on the floor, writhing, as if movement would stem the flow.

Warton's breath, punctuated with sobs and gurgles as he both bled and choked to death, lasted about three minutes. Slowly, his arms slumped to the floor and the man was still.

Two minutes later, the man's heart stopped beating and the blood flow began to diminish until there was hardly anything left in his veins.

Neither man paid any heed to the dead body.

"Let's empty that safe an' get the hell outta here," Dent said.

Both men grabbed the sacks of money from the safe and Dent, opening the rear of the bank, began tossing the sacks onto the buckboard. It took them no more than five minutes to clear the safe — including the cashiers' trays.

Dent took the reins and the two men, the woman, the dead man and, of course, the money, left Woebegone.

9

DOUG SANDERS yawned, stretched and got out of his portable crib. Although the night air was cold, the atmosphere inside his tent was cloying, stuffy and warm.

The water in the basin resting atop a wooden table was warm when he placed both hands in it to splash his face in an effort to wake himself up.

It didn't work. He called for cold water. The cook, a Chinaman, brought a pail of cold water in, threw the warm away and refilled the basin. Sanders splashed his face again, this time the shock of the cold water really brought him round.

He dried himself off and took out his pocket watch: ten thirty. Excellent! he said out loud. With a meeting with Dent and Bore at eleven, he had enough time to get himself ready, maybe a light snack and a glass of wine.

The herd was due to move out at sunrise, a deal Sanders had come to with the herd's previous owners. Although not paid for yet, Sanders' letters of credit were good enough for them. The actual transfer of paper money would be at noon.

By that time, Sanders figured, the herd should be thirty to forty miles west of Woebegone; his alibi complete.

He changed his shirt, put on a tie and jacket and sat the table, waiting for his food. Those two bums had better show up, he thought, they were vital to his plan.

Locklin entered the tent to get his final instructions — it only took a matter of moments.

"You're sure everything is in place?" Sanders asked.

"Positive. Nothing'll go wrong, jus' as long as Dent and Bore do their bit."

"Good. We'll meet up on the trail. Good luck, Mr Locklin." Sanders nodded, but didn't offer his hand.

Last Chance Locklin tipped his hat and left the tent; he was on his way to Woebegone.

A plate of food and a glass of wine was placed in front of Sanders and, smiling, he tucked in.

★ ★ ★

"Two men," Crooked Grin said. "Plenty tracks."

Crooked Grin walked towards the door and went outside. "See, wheel marks. Arrive lighter than they leave. Ruts deeper."

For the life of him, Tom Hilks would never have noticed that, but now that Crooked Grin had pointed it out, they were as plain as the nose on his face.

"You reckon they took the body away?" he asked Crooked Grin.

"Yes. Trail leads back, I follow."

"Sheriff! Sheriff! You better come

140

quick!" A man's voice broke through the gloom. "The bank, it's the bank!"

Tom Hilks wasted no time on questions. He left Crooked Grin to follow the wheel tracks and ran back into the street.

Eighty yards further on, a dull red glow came from the inside of the bank.

"Shit!" Tom whispered hoarsely under his breath.

"Get some men, we need water, an' we need it now!"

The man, one of the drovers, ran straight to the saloon while Tom headed for the bank building. Inside, he heard the crackle of flame; pretty soon, he knew, the entire building could explode in flame. The wood was as dry as a bone and twice as volatile.

He stood outside the front door of the building, and that's when he noticed the splintered wood on the boardwalk. The door had been broken in.

Tom tried the handle, but the door

was firmly locked from the inside. He took out his sideiron and, using the butt, he smashed the window.

Immediately, a billow of smoke greeted him even before the glass had finished falling to the ground. Tom tied his bandanna round his mouth and nose and, feeling for the inside bolts, he released them and entered the bank.

The smoke, though thick, didn't fill the entire room. It seemed to be coming from the far corner. The corner where Henry Warton had his fine desk.

Tom began making his way across the room, behind him, two men had entered with buckets. "Over here," Tom called out, and the two men threw the water in his direction, soaking him to the skin.

"Not over me you idiots!" Tom yelled, but the two men had gone to be replaced by another two. "Here," Tom said again, "Bring the water over here!"

This time the men came forward

and waited until they could see the source of the smoke before emptying the contents of the buckets.

Tom heard the sizzle and saw steam rise into the air as the water hit. The area of the fire was small and was all but extinguished, but the smoke was thicker now, and white as it fought to stay in existence.

"Get some more water and bring lamps," Tom ordered as the original two men returned. "Throw the water over the desk," Tom said to them, "not over me again!"

"Sure thing, Sheriff," they replied and did as they were ordered.

The smoke thinned way down now and Tom saw Henry Warton lying by the open safe.

"Jesus, Joseph and Mary," he said under his breath and went forward to Warton's side.

Although not a medical man, Tom Hilks knew a dead man when he saw one. Down on one knee, Tom could see that Warton's throat had been cut practically from ear to ear.

"Goddamn!" he said aloud. Standing, he then felt his left knee, it was soggy, soggy with the blood of the dead man. Taking his bandanna off, he rubbed at his trouser leg as if it were full of scorpions.

The two drovers who'd drenched Tom initially were joined by the other two. "Shit in hell!" one of them said.

"Sheriff," another called out. "I think you better see this."

Tom walked across to the safe: it was, of course, empty.

Crooked Grin walked into the bank from the unlocked rear door. "Tracks lead here, then away," he said. Then he noticed Henry Warton lying on the floor and the open safe. "Whoever killed man in bunkhouse, killed this man too."

"Are there enough tracks to follow?" Tom asked.

"Always enough tracks to follow," Crooked Grin said.

"Then, by the powers invested in me,

etc, etc, I swear you all in as deputies. Okay?"

"First time for everything," Crooked Grin said.

"Two of us'll be okay, Sheriff," one of the men said, "but we still got a herd to take care of. Even though it looks like we ain't gonna git paid."

"Fair enough," Tom said. "Let's get saddled and ride out."

"Don't I get badge?" Crooked Grin asked.

"Ain't got time, I'll fetch you one later, all right?"

Crooked Grin was crestfallen, but he nodded.

"Be grateful if one of you could go get Harold Meeks, he's actin' mayor, an' ask him to organize some people to clear this place up and see to the body," Tom said as he made his way to the door.

"Sure thing, Sheriff," the man replied and followed them out the door.

145

★ ★ ★

The ride out to Aggie Miller's shack took only half an hour and Dent began to wonder whether it was far enough away from town but, as they didn't have their horses and they certainly didn't relish the idea of heading out into the desert at night, they had little choice.

The bumpy trail and the speed the buckboard travelled brought Aggie round again. This time, her head thumped like drum beats and she was glad of the darkness as she doubted she could focus properly. She was being tossed around like a rag-doll in the back of the buckboard, still tied hand and foot and a filthy rag tied across her mouth, she was, nevertheless, pleased to be alive.

The thoughts of poor old Charlie filled her head and she was glad not to have seen the old man die.

Trying to get her thoughts in order proved harder than Aggie would have realized. Almost blind with the pain and blackness, and physically helpless, she tried to concentrate, but found it useless. Her mind wandered off of its own accord.

Driving over a particularly rutted piece of the trail, Aggie's entire body left the buckboard for an instant, before thumping back down again. But the bumpy trail had done some good: her head was free of the sacking and she could see, albeit blurrily, the stars overhead in the deep-blue of the night sky. She concentrated on those, getting her head back in order.

On and on they went and to Aggie, it seemed like they'd been driving for hours. She ached in every part of her body, but at least, she thought, I still *have* every part of my body.

With a suddenness that rocked her, the buckboard ground to a halt and she heard the voices of two men. Voices she both recognized and feared.

Turning her head to one side she came face to face with the lifeless head of old Charlie, the slit in his throat all too apparent and his dead eyes staring at her blankly.

Despite the gag, Aggie screamed. She didn't stop screaming until she fainted, and even then, she screamed inside.

★ ★ ★

Saddled now and ready to ride, Tom, Crooked Grin and the two drovers left town. They headed north following the wheel tracks with Crooked Grin leading. At times, Tom couldn't even see the ground, let alone follow a trail, but Crooked Grin led unerringly. The longer they rode, the nearer they got to Aggie's place.

In Tom's vest pocket was the piece of blue material he'd found; he fingered it, lovingly, and a steely expression filled his face. Determination led him to the woman he loved. He only prayed to God she was alive and unharmed.

★ ★ ★

Last Chance Locklin and his band of three hand-picked gunmen stopped on the outskirts of Woebegone. In the distance, they could see smoke rising into the air, but there wasn't much and so they dismissed it from their thoughts.

It was exactly ten forty-five.

Locklin dismounted and the other three men followed suit. They had an hour to kill, maybe more, so Locklin decided they might as well get comfortable.

"How come we's stopping here?" one of the men asked.

"So's I can keep an eye on the town," Locklin said without looking at the speaker. "I need to make sure it's asleep afore we go in."

The man didn't say any more. He was being well paid, so what the hell?

Locklin removed the saddle from his horse and told another man to stand guard and keep an eye on the town.

149

"What am I lookin' fer?" the man asked.

"Silence," Locklin replied. "I want to know when the town goes to bed. Okay?"

"Sure, you're the boss."

"Yeah," Locklin replied, getting himself comfortable, "I'm the boss."

★ ★ ★

"You know somethin'?" Dent said.

"No. What?" Bore said.

"I reckon we hide this here loot an' them two a-ways out in the desert, afore we ride out to that Mr Sanders an' see what it is he wants us to do."

"Hell an' damnation!" Bore spat. "Every time I think to gettin' to grips with a woman, we's gotta do somethin' else."

"Can't be helped," Dent said. "We'll have plenty o' time fer her."

"We sure as hell better have," Bore said sulkily.

The terrain behind Aggie's shack was rocky, a gentle slope leading up to a plateau some two-hundred feet high.

Dent looked at the skyline: "Reckon that's as good a place as we'll find," he said pointing upwards.

"You mean carry 'em up there?" Bore was incredulous.

"Sure. We may be back late, who knows. Better hide 'em good, else they could be found," Dent said.

"Shit!" Bore spat heavily into the dirt.

"Come on, let's git goin'," Dent grabbed hold of four money bags and began climbing. Bore sat for a while, trying to come up with a better idea but, as usual, he failed.

He jumped to the ground and gathered the rest of the bags together, holding them in one hand, then he roughly picked up the body of Charlie and slung him over his shoulder and trudged up the slope after Dent.

Nearing the top, Dent spotted a

small cave almost hidden by brush. He stopped and peered in. It was pitch black and he didn't want to throw the money bags into what could turn out to be a bottomless pit.

He lit a match and stared hard, the cave wasn't large, it was just a small hole, maybe two feet deep, but big enough to hide the money. Dent waited 'til Bore arrived and together they stowed the money safely.

"I'll git the gal," Dent said. "See what lies ahead an' join you."

Bore spat, saying nothing. He watched as Dent went down the slope, then he turned and carried on climbing.

It took him five more minutes to reach the plateau, where he dumped the body of Charlie down on the rock and waited for Dent. Three minutes later, Dent appeared over the rise with Aggie on his shoulders. He gently lowered her to the ground, then both men gathered brush and twigs until they reckoned the two bodies were well out of sight. Then, wordlessly, they returned to the buckboard and set off for the campsite of Doug Sanders.

Each man was alone with his thoughts and both men's thoughts were on Aggie.

★ ★ ★

Crooked Grin reined to a halt outside Aggie's shack. The tracks stopped here, and Crooked Grin dropped from his horse and inspected them closely.

"They unload here," he said. Then he walked forwards to the slope of rocks. "Maybe take up there."

"But where'd the wagon go?" Tom asked.

"Wagon gone south again," he pointed at the only vaguely visible weel ruts.

"Goddamn!" Tom said.

"Goddamn, indeed," Crooked Grin replied. "We go after wagon, or climb rocks?"

Tom sat atop his horse: he had a tough decision to make. Should he let the riders on the wagon, killers, ride off? Or should he let his heart rule his head.

Tom sat and the others watched and waited.

10

HAROLD and a couple of the boys took Henry Warton's body over to the livery stable. On finding it locked, they took it round the rear by the cow pens and left it on a covered wagon awaiting the ministrations of Crooked Grin.

By now, word had got round Woebegone that the bank had been robbed, Aggie Miller had disappeared and the whole town dang near burned down.

A small knot of people gathered outside the bank — not that they had a great deal of money deposited, nor because Warton was dead. They were just curious. Rumours spread: the most ridiculous being that Aggie Miller had robbed the bank and hightailed to Los Angeles with the cattle money.

Several of the drovers were also

gathered there, they'd helped put the fire out and carry Warton's body away, now they were getting a mite angry as they suddenly realized their wages were in the bank.

There wasn't much Harold Meeks could do now, leastways, not until Tom returned, hopefully with Aggie. He'd left his wife at home, dead bodies not being the sort of thing a married woman should get involved with.

So, after going through Henry's pockets and taking the keys to the bank, Harold locked up and went home.

Pretty soon, the group of people began to lose interest and dispersed, some to keep the cows company, the rest to the saloon.

Last Chance Locklin leaned up on one elbow and drew a cheroot from a tube he kept in his shirt pocket. Striking a match, he lit up and inhaled deeply.

He looked up at the sky — thick and black, peppered with stars and a quarter moon shining as best it could — and felt the cold breeze wash over his face.

"Any sign o' movement in town?" he called out to the lookout.

"Naw, pretty quiet now. Street's clear, a few in the saloon. That's about it."

Locklin inhaled again and made his mind up: "Okay, let's git this thing done."

He threw his unfinished cheroot to the ground and stood, stretching the stiffness in his legs and back, before mounting his horse.

"Check your guns," he bellowed, "I don't want no shootin', but I want you ready if'n needs be."

Mounted, the four riders set off at a walk towards Woebegone. They were in no hurry. They had all the time in the world.

★ ★ ★

Tom Hilks also made his mind up. He reasoned, if Aggie and maybe Charlie

157

were dead, he'd waste valuable time in finding that out. If Aggie was alive, well, he figured she could hang on while he tracked down the bank-robbing killers and brought them to justice. Then he'd go back for her — alone.

"Let's go," was all he said as he wheeled his mount round.

"We follow buckboard?" Crooked Grin asked.

"We follow buckboard," Tom said and kicked the flanks of his horse and set off at a gallop.

The tracks led a wide loop round Woebegone, following the east trail. Slowing down, to give Crooked Grin a better chance of keeping the tracks in sight, he asked: "Where the hell are they headin'?"

"Not know," Crooked Grin replied, "but soon we find out."

They rode in silence for another five minutes before Crooked Grin suddenly reined his animal in. He sat rock-still in his saddle, it looked as if he were smelling the air.

Tom had noticed the wind had picked up, but he paid it no attention, the wind often did as it swept across the desert floor. But now that they'd stopped riding, the howl of the wind, louder, it seemed in the distance, began to unnerve him.

"Sand devil comes dancing this way," Crooked Grin said.

"Goddamn it to hell an' back," Tom said.

Crooked Grin had already dismounted. Bringing the reins over his horse's head, he tied a cloth over the animal's eyes to protect them from the stinging sand he knew was only minutes away.

Tom and the rest of the posse followed suit. Crooked Grin then grabbed the reins of all the horses and tied them together, nose to nose, so that the animals formed a circle. They'd be less restless that way.

"Take saddles and bedrolls," Crooked Grin ordered.

The men didn't need asking twice.

The wind had practically doubled in strength in the last ten minutes, the distant howling was much closer now and the sand began to lift into the air, being sucked up by the hungry wind.

Sage brush and tumbleweed clattered past the group of men as they sat huddled behind their saddles, blankets and bedrolls covering them. But still the sand seeped in, clogging nose and eyes and ears, filling their mouths with grit.

There was no way they'd be able to follow *any* tracks now.

The moon and stars were the first to disappear, blotted out by the huge cloud of sand that seemed to be trying to take off any exposed flesh as it was whipped along by the wind.

Tom tried calling to Crooked Grin, but the howling wind drowned out any question he might have asked. All he wanted to know was how long would this last?

Crooked Grin was wondering the same thing.

Sand began to build up around the saddles, soon they would be covered and then, in their turn, the men. As long as they kept an air passage open, they'd be all right and once the sand built up, the force of the wind would be lost on them.

Tom Hilks resigned himself to staying put until the wind blew itself out, or moved further on. He suddenly wished he'd gone up the plateau instead, at least he'd have the comfort — hopefully — of knowing Aggie was alive. But now — in this storm — exposed on the plateau, he shuddered to think.

★ ★ ★

For the third time that day, Aggie opened her eyes to blackness. This time, a howling gale accompanied the dark. She wriggled and writhed on the hard rock, trying to free her face once more from the sacking that still enveloped her. Succeeding, she wished she'd stayed covered up.

The moon had disappeared, but, higher up as they were, there was little sand to blow around. The most shocking sight she had to confront was the face — and neck — of old Charlie, lying next to her.

She knew a sand storm when she saw one, they blew up out of nothing and seemed to be able to last for days or hours, there was no way of telling. The howling gale thrashed wildly all around her and there wasn't a damn thing she could do about it.

Already, her lips and tongue felt swollen, the effect of the gag and the fact that she'd not drunk anything now for over five hours, was beginning to sap at her strength.

Her jaw was painful to move as she tried to ascertain if it was broken and from the vision of her left eye, she could see a swollen cheek as she looked down her nose. Still, she thought again, I'm alive.

It was getting difficult to swallow. Saliva soaked into the gag but there seemed none in her mouth. If there was a hell, thought Aggie, then I'm plum in the middle of it. She closed her eyes against the cold wind — she could only wait for either the two men to return, which seemed unlikely, or daybreak, which seemed just too far away.

★ ★ ★

Dent and Bore made it to the campsite with minutes to spare. The wind had picked up speed and although they weren't concerned overly, they knew that unless they reached Sanders' place before the storm broke, they might not make it until dawn.

All hell had broken loose as they arrived. The large tent was all but flying away as Sanders' crew, unused to winds of this velocity, had been a tad slow in loosening off the ropes and taking the tent down. Dent and Bore saw six or seven men battling to contain the canvas that began to look like a giant kite that would whisk them away at any second.

Pulling the buckboard to a halt, Bore unhitched the team and led them across the compound to bed them down with the other horses that were tied to a rope in the lee of some rocks. At least they'd be out of the main onslaught there, he thought.

Returning to the buckboard, Bore and Dent, with the aid of two other hands, managed to tip it on its side, thereby giving them shelter.

Sanders, seeing what the men had achieved, left the flapping tent and, grabbing blankets and a bedroll, ran across to the makeshift shelter.

"Welcome to the desert, Mr Sanders," Dent said and then covered his nose and mouth with a bandanna.

Seeing this, and without replying, Sanders followed suit, except his mask was a white handkerchief that looked as if it'd never been used before.

"Guess we're holed up awhiles," Bore shouted, but the wind seemed to whip the words out of his mouth and throw them away.

"Say what?" Dent bellowed.

Bore shook his head, it was useless to try and say anything.

The wind speed picked up even more as the group of men huddled behind the buckboard, the tent gave a last, lingering attempt to stay put before the gale picked it up and it flew off into the darkness, quickly followed by the contents of the washroom, the bedroom and anything that hadn't been nailed down to the ground.

There was nothing anyone could do, except sit and wait.

★ ★ ★

Locklin and his men hit town just before the wind picked up speed. Already, though, a tumbleweed derby was taking place in the main street, and above the noise of the wind, the creaking of the buildings filled the air.

The cattle, afeared as they were at being penned up, and now found that they were stuck where they were, began a low incessant bellow, that added to the nightmarish scene.

The saloon was the only building that showed any signs of life, that and the house down the street aways, but Locklin was sure that, if this was going to be a sand-storm, no one would venture out until the wind blew itself out.

Leading his men round the side of the bank building, he dismounted and tethered his animal. The alleyway, in the lee of the wind, would be more than a safe place for the animals. Besides, he thought, the noise of the wind would drown out any noise he and his men might make — would make.

Locklin smiled to himself; things couldn't have worked out better. They could take as long as they wanted robbing the bank and then skidoodle down the trail at sun-up, while Woebegone slept.

The sticks of dynamite and fuses in

his saddlebags felt heavy as he lifted them down and slung the bag over his shoulder. Pointing, he led the way to the rear of the bank.

All the while, the wind howled as it neared the town and sand began dancing in the dark alleyway.

Locklin pointed, and one of his men, axe in hand, began chopping at the rear door. It took him less than five minutes to splinter the wooden door and gain access.

Inside, the smell of smoke was quickly whipped away by the wind, and Locklin paid it no heed. He walked straight across the room to the big, black safe and placed his saddlebag on the floorboards. Unhooking the clasp, he lovingly removed each stick of dynamite one by one, then he began to cut the fuses, each one four or five inches in length. Then he plugged the top of each stick of dynamite with a length of fuse and, mounting some at the base of the safe, and two more by the lock mechanism, he stood and surveyed the room.

"Move that desk on its side," he ordered, pointing at Henry Warton's pride and joy.

Two men tipped the desk on its side facing the safe. When Locklin was sure everything was ready, he sat behind the desk with his men.

"You ain't lit the fuses," one of the men said.

"Nope," Locklin replied. "I figured I'd wait a few more minutes, let the wind pick up, help to drown out the noise."

As if at his command, the wind did just that. The men looked at Locklin and then at each other as the big man struck a match and lit a cheroot. Inhaling leisurely, he stood and walked towards the safe.

Using the glowing cheroot, he touched each of the fuses in turn — eight in all — made sure they were all burning, then strolled back behind the desk where he sat and continued to smoke.

The men, arms over their heads or with fingers in their ears, sat and waited — they didn't have long to wait.

The explosion, when it came, was earsplittingly deafening. The force moved the solid-wood desk backwards, crashing down on the men behind it, fortunately, for them, the legs didn't break off as the desk righted itself above them.

Paper and splinters of wood still fell to the ground as the wind seemed to shoot straight through the bank. As the smoke and dust settled, it was easy to see why.

The dynamite had lifted the safe off its base and thrown it backwards, through the wood wall, and out into the alleyway. The wind, never one to miss an opportunity, now blew in the back door and straight out the other side, creating a tunnel through which sand and anything else blew.

The noise of the wind was now almost as deafening as the explosion had been, and for the first time in his life, doubt flooded through Locklin.

Shit, I hope I didn't use too much o' the damn stuff, he thought as he stood up to view the havoc created by both dynamite and wind.

Through the gloom, he saw the giant safe, lying on its back, the door missing altogether and papers were flying out of it every whichway.

"Quick!" he shouted, "the wind's stealing the money!"

The men raced to the hole in the wood wall and gawped when they saw the inside of the safe.

It was empty!

11

WOEBEGONE really lived up to its name that night. The storm raged and ranted until the small hours of the morning, which didn't affect most folks, except waking them up every now and then as something the wind had torn loose from one building banged into another.

As the first watery fingers of dawn crept along the desert floor, the posse were digging themselves out of the mound of sand and debris that had built up around them during the night.

"Hellfire," Tom muttered, spitting sand from his mouth. "That sure was the mother of all storms."

The other men could say nothing but agree.

Crooked Grin had, God knows how, managed to find enough wood to start a fire and already the coffee pot was bubbling away.

"Tracks all gone," he said unnecessarily.

"Well, that figures," Tom replied. "We'll just head out towards Sanders' camp. I'm sure that's where they was a-goin' anyways."

Silently, the men drank their coffee. The first mouthfuls they spat out, using the scalding black liquid to get rid of the sand that seemed to have crept into everywhere.

Crooked Grin took the bandannas off the horses, who seemed none the worse for their night out in the storm. Within fifteen minutes, with the sun hanging low on the horizon, the men set off once again.

The frustration of the wasted night hung heavily on Tom Hilks's shoulders. He fervently wished he'd climbed the plateau the night before, at least now he'd know whether Aggie was alive or — He stopped his thoughts in mid track. There was no way he was going to think of that last word.

* * *

Locklin and his gang were at a loss. Where the hell had the money gone?

They'd spent the whole night sheltering in the bank: it seemed pointless trying to ride through the storm — besides, no one would be out on a night like that!

Locklin's plan was to join up with the drive, that way they'd melt into the background and no one would take much notice of them.

The herd had been restless all night and on more than one occasion, the panic that went through the herd almost manifested in a stampede. The corral held firm, much to the relief of the drovers, any breakout would have cost dearly as it would have been almost impossible to round them up again.

Locklin led his men across to the rear of the livery stable, helped themselves to coffee and watched as the corrals were opened up, and the long, slow, journey to Los Angeles began.

There was almost as much dust floating around now as there had been the night before.

"What the hell do we do now?" one of the riders asked Locklin.

"Beats me. Someone's robbed the bank, that's for sure. Thing is, who?"

"Sanders won't believe us. He'll figure we stole it fer ourselves," the man voiced what they were all feeling.

"Well, we'll just have to convince him otherwise," Locklin said and the firm set of his jaw and his steely expression stopped all further discussion.

It took nearly an hour to get the herd in line and on the road. Normally, townsfolk would be out whistling and cheering as they left, but this morning, the town was empty. Folks were more concerned with fixing up damage to their houses or shops to pay the herd much attention.

Clem Watkins was the only person watching as the herd left town. He'd been up most of the night with the storm, helping the drovers keep the herd calm, and doing running repairs on wind damage.

The saloon had lost part of its roof, it was lucky the wind hadn't ripped the whole thing off, but Clem had been there, hammer and nails ready.

"Anyone seen my son?" he called out as the drovers began leaving.

He got a negative response from everyone he asked. Most were too busy with their job to pay him much heed.

Clem got to wondering where Crooked Grin had got to. It wasn't like him to just disappear without leaving a note or at least waking him up.

He checked through the livery stable, in case Crooked Grin was asleep somewhere, but he wasn't. He'd already searched through their house so his next port of call was Harold Meeks, acting town mayor.

"'Mornin' Clem," Harold said as he opened his front door.

"'Mornin', Harold. You seen Crooked Grin?"

"Not since he rode off with Tom," Harold said.

"Rode off? What for?" Clem asked.

Harold proceeded to tell him of the events of the previous evening in graphic detail.

"How the hell did I miss out on all that?" Clem said.

"Beats me, Clem. Come on in, Sadie's got the coffee on. I've jus' bin checkin' on the storm damage."

"Anything I can do to help?"

"Hell, no. Fixed up most myself, weren't much."

"So there's no news of Aggie Miller then?" Clem finally asked.

"None. Doubt they got far, though. Storm was too bad. Doubt Tom even caught up with 'em."

"Wonder if I should maybe mosey on out an' see what I can find out?" Clem said.

"I could ride with you," Harold said.

"You ain't going nowhere," Sadie said quickly. "Tom asked you to stay here an' take care o' things 'til he got back. Now, if Clem wants to go ridin' off into the desert, that's his business, but you ain't going nowhere!"

"Looks like I'll go alone," Clem said, a wry grin on his face.

"Now see here, Sadie — " Harold began.

"See here nothin'!" Sadie said and slammed two mugs of coffee down on the table.

"Well, looks like I'm in charge o' the town, Clem. I'd better wait here for Tom."

Clem smiled and sipped his coffee.

★ ★ ★

Doug Sanders had spent the most uncomfortable night of his life. He'd hardly been able to get a wink of sleep. Uppermost in his mind was choking to death — and that was enough to keep any one awake all night.

As the storm abated, Sanders quickly got his men into action. The camp was cleared up, ready for the off. They managed to find the tent, but most of the interior was lost, probably come to light the next time there was a storm.

The cook managed to drum up some breakfast, he'd spent the night in the food locker, making sure it stayed where it was — no greater love hath man than his stomach.

Breakfast over, Sanders sent the wagons on ahead. He still had business to attend to with Dent and Bore.

"Now, gentlemen," he began. "Are you ready to work?" he asked.

"'Pends what it is," Dent said cautiously.

"What it is," Sanders went on, "is this. A lot of my money is tied up in the bank, and I want to withdraw it."

The sarcasm of the remark was lost on Dent and Bore.

"Why don' you jus' go git it," Bore said.

"You miss the point, gentlemen. I've hired you two for that purpose."

"I don' follow," Dent said.

"I want you to rob the bank!" Sanders said.

"But — " Bore began before Dent's boot reached his shin bone.

"What the hell you do that fer?" Bore bellowed.

"Just crossin' ma legs," Dent said.

"You understand now?" Sanders continued.

"We sure do," Dent said.

"Well," Sanders pulled out a piece of paper from his inside pocket. "Warton opens up at nine-thirty, precisely. You are to be there when he arrives, which is at eight-forty-five. You have thirty minutes to persuade him to open the safe before the rest of the staff arrive."

"'Sposin' he don't want to open up the safe," Dent said.

"I'm sure you can help him change his mind," Sanders said.

"What's in it fer us?" Dent asked, scratching the stubble on his chin.

"A thousand dollars each, and a job in Los Angeles for as long as you like."

Dent looked at Bore. His expression told Bore to keep his big mouth shut.

Bore did.

"Okay. You got yerself a deal," Dent said.

"And just in case you get any ideas of maybe keeping the money," Sanders went on, "you will be watched, most carefully, by some of my men. You won't know who they are, or where they are. But they'll be there. There will be no escape."

Dent grinned. "Mister, we may be saddlebums and low-lifes to you, but we got our code!"

"Yeah," Bore added, "we got our code."

"Good. So have I," Sanders said. "So have I."

Dent and Bore hitched up the team for the ride back to Woebegone, or at least, in that direction. Sanders watched them leave. His plan was working fine. All he had to do now was wait by the river for Locklin to bring the money and the plan would be complete. He'd have the cattle and his money back.

Perfect.

★ ★ ★

Aggie Miller had slept all through the storm. The rocky plateau had sheltered her from the worst of the winds and sand and, as there was precious little she could do, she slept.

Her mouth was badly swollen and the pain in her jaw had intensified during the night, but she'd been so exhausted, there was no way it would keep her awake. Now, the pain throbbed in her head and her hands and feet were totally numb.

She once more began moving her hands and fingers, trying to get the circulation going. Her shoulders too were stiff and sore, but she ignored them. If she stood a chance of breaking free, she had to have the use of her hands.

The pain in her jaw was quickly

forgotten as the pain in her hands took over. Aggie screamed out loud, she saw no point in putting on a brave face, besides, when you scream in the desert, no one can hear you.

Slowly, painfully, feeling returned to her hands and she began moving her feet. The ropes had burned into her flesh during the night but the sores were just a dull ache and, summoning up her inner strength, she ignored them. She had to get free before the two men returned. Assuming they would.

The thought that they might not filled Aggie with a terror she'd not known before. To die here, alone with Charlie, was something she'd fight against with her last breath.

Little did Aggie realize that the storm had probably saved her life. The creatures of the night, coyotes in the main, were also holed up, unable to hunt for food. And although they mostly hunted at night, the pangs of hunger now forced them out of their lairs in the never-ending search for food.

Nature's other cleaners, vultures, also had the smell of death pinpointed. It was said a vulture could detect a carcass a hundred miles distant. True or not, Aggie watched in horror as the early morning sky filled with the long, black, gliding wings of the huge birds as they circled high overhead.

Charlie's body, lying not more than three feet away, stank. Aggie was surprised she hadn't noticed it before. Realization that the vultures could also smell it determined her to move as far away as she was able.

Slowly, painfully, she began to roll over and over. Each turn was like torture, racking her body with pain. But the alternative — being pecked to death in a frenzy of feeding — drove her on. Five feet, six, seven. Bit by bit, she distanced herself from Charlie's body. Ten feet, eleven, twelve, the distance grew and as it did, the birds circled lower.

Aggie couldn't smell Charlie any more; she had to crane her neck now just to be able to see his lifeless form and, although the pain was now intense, she continued to roll away.

The skin on her face was beginning to peel off as she repeatedly came into contact with the unforgiving rock, but she kept going. The sacking protected the rest of her body and for the first time, she was grateful for that as, where Dent had ripped her dress, her breasts and stomach would have been torn to shreds.

Exhausted, Aggie rested, her breath coming in short pants as the gag made it almost impossible to breathe through her mouth. Sweat coursed down her face and she tried to blink it out of her eyes, but as fast as she cleared her vision, the sweat rolled in again until she felt she was looking at the world from inside a barrel of water.

She stayed perfectly still, her chest rising and falling as she fought to regain control. Lying on her back, the warmth of the sun began to filter through, hitting her face first, and gently seeping through the sacking. She hadn't even realized she'd been shaking with cold for last twenty minutes.

She closed her eyes and her breath began to even out and as she relaxed, so the aches and pains returned with a vengeance. Hearing noises, her eyes opened in alarm.

The birds had landed.

★ ★ ★

Clem Watkins saddled up and rode his horse out of the livery stable. Harold would keep an eye on it for him until he, or Crooked Grin, returned.

He sat atop his mount, resting his hands on the pommel. Which way to ride? he wondered. He looked up at the blue sky, white wisps of clouds skittered high up, the sun, a bright yellow-red disc burning away the moisture, what little there was, no sign of the previous night's storm. Clem lowered his eyes back to ground level, seeing the sand piled up everywhere in small dunes, the slight damage to buildings being the only evidence and that would soon set itself to rights.

Gazing towards the distant horizon, Clem saw the black spots circling high up. Buzzards, he thought. Now they don't congregate like that for nothing. His direction chosen, he cantered out of Woebegone, keeping his eyes trained on the small, black dots.

12

"I DON'T unnerstand," Bore said as they rode out of Sanders' camp. "What the hell does he wanna rob his own money fer?"

Dent reined in the buckboard, tipped his Stetson higher on his head and looked blankly at Bore.

"Sometimes," he said, "I don't think you got the brains the good Lord gave when you was born."

"Say what!"

"Well, let's see if'n you can figure it out. Sanders buys a herd o' beef, right? An' he pays good money for 'em, right?"

"Yeah."

"Then he robs the bank, you with me still?"

"Er — yeah."

"Good. Now. He's still got the cows *an'* now he's got his money back to boot!"

Bore's face screwed up in heavy

concentration: "Right!"

"Good."

"But we done robbed the bank already."

"I *knows* that, but Sanders doesn't!"

"But he soon will if'n we don't ride in with the money," Bore said.

"We ain't ridin' in wi' no money," Dent replied. "We's gonna ride back to town, pick us up our horses, ride on to the plateau, git the money and ride on out o' this territory as quick as we can. You got it?"

"'Course I got it, I ain't stupid!"

"Right, let's go."

Dent grabbed the buffalo-hide whip and geed the horses on. The going wasn't easy. The storm had blown sand across the trail and the horses were having a tough time keeping going.

In the distance, they saw a dust cloud.

"Shit an' hellfire!" Dent said. "I plum forgot the herd."

"They won't be a-headin' this a-ways," Bore said.

"How'd you figure that?" Dent asked.

"Easy. River's due west. Cattle'll need waterin' afore sunset. They gotta go that way."

Dent looked at Bore. What he said made sense.

"Okay, let's ride around it." So saying, they made a slight detour, trying to keep the team on the harder packed sand.

The howling winds of the night before had settled back to being just a breeze again. But the breeze was blowing directly in their faces and as they neared the drive, the air was filled with dust and grit, making the journey uncomfortable. Covering their faces, the two men drove on to Woebegone.

Successfully rounding the herd, they entered town from the north and reined in at the livery stable. The doors were wide open but there was no one there.

Leaving the buckboard outside, the team busy lapping up water from the

189

trough, they saddled up and headed off in a matter of minutes.

Harold Meeks saw them ride out.

★ ★ ★

Locklin had made up his mind. He decided to ride on and confront Sanders. Something wasn't panning out here. Either Sanders was lying, or he was trying to set Locklin and his men up — either way, he intended to find out.

Leaving his men behind, he set off to where he knew Sanders last was, shouldn't be difficult to follow the trail and catch up with him. He told his men to stay with the herd and that he'd return before noon.

They watched as he set off. None of them doubted his word.

It took Locklin an hour to spot the wagons of Sanders' camp lumbering along the trail heading for the river and the meeting place. Spurring his animal on, Locklin soon caught them up.

"Ah," Sanders said, "Mr Locklin, good to see you."

"I ain't that sure," Locklin said.

"I beg your pardon?"

"I said, I ain't so sure. We raided the bank las' night, jus' like you ordered, only someone beat us to it!"

Sanders went purple with rage.

"You puttin' me on?" all semblance of his fine, fancy talk disappeared.

"Do I look as if I am?"

Sanders looked deeply into Locklin's eyes, then looked away. "No. No, it doesn't," he said, calming himself down.

"What gives?" Locklin asked.

"What gives, Mr Locklin, is that I've been double-crossed."

"By who?"

"I can only guess that those two saddlebums had more goin' for 'em than I gave 'em credit for."

"The two you hired to rob the bank after we done it?"

"The very same."

"Where are they now?" Locklin asked

through gritted teeth.

"Back to town, I guess," Sanders said. "You want some men?"

"No. I can deal with them myself."

Without another word, Locklin wheeled around and galloped off towards Woebegone, death in his eyes.

Sanders watched him go. He sat and thought and then decided on a plan of action. Getting three men together, he left the wagon train and set off for Woebegone.

He'd decided he didn't trust anybody, and there was no way he was going to be implicated — in anything.

★ ★ ★

It was Crooked Grin who first heard the sound of the cattle moving off. Dismounting, he placed his fingers and an ear to the ground.

Tom sat and watched before asking: "What gives?"

"Herd on move." He stayed where he was, eyes closed in utter concentration.

"Riders," he said suddenly. "Buckboard heading back to town!"

"How the hell do you know that?" Tom asked.

Crooked Grin said only: "I know."

"Okay, let's ride!" Without waiting for Crooked Grin to mount up, Tom Hilks dug his heels in and they galloped off towards Woebegone. It didn't take Crooked Grin long to catch up and, within fifteen minutes, they arrived in town.

Harold Meeks, brushing sand off the boardwalk in front of his store greeted them as they arrived.

"Any news?"

"Yes, and no," Tom said. "But first, you seen anyone come in on a buckboard?"

"Sure. 'Bout thirty minutes ago, headed off south by horse," he answered.

"Right, let's go," Tom said.

"There was another fella, too. That fella who killed Hank Bryan. Now what was his name? Locklin, Last Chance Locklin.

"See'd him in town las' night, too. Just afore the storm, him an' three men looked in at the bank. Didn't think much of it at the time, seein' as there was no money in there anyways," Harold said.

"Wind started to blow up, an' I knew what was comin', so I went home to be with Sadie."

"They still in town?" Tom asked.

"Nope. Saw 'em leavin' with the drive this mornin', that's why I was surprised when Locklin appeared agen."

"Thanks, Harold. Stay put, we'll be back."

The four riders set off once more. "Seems like we was destined to reach that plateau," Tom called out to Crooked Grin.

The Indian remained silent.

Tom rode silently now, alone with his thoughts. Not just about Aggie, but Locklin was now included.

The man was employed by Sanders. What the hell was the connection? He certainly wasn't one of the two men

Aggie had described. So how was he tied up in all this?

Four men dead. One definitely by Locklin, the other three? Well, could've been done by anyone, but Tom wasn't so sure about that.

If Charlie was dead, was it by the same men who'd tried to rape Aggie? Were they the same men who'd kidnapped her now?

Tom Hilks's head began to swim. He had so many questions and not nearly enough answers.

Pulling his mount over closer to Crooked Grin, Tom asked: "Where'd they get that buckboard from?"

"Me."

"Why the hell didn' you say so in the first place?"

"Me thought you knew that."

"Hell! Can you describe them?"

"Only one man. The man known as Bore," and Crooked Grin described the same man Aggie had described earlier the day before.

"Bore? Wild Man Bore?"

"I know only Bore."

"So that's it. They must've loaded Charlie onto the buckboard with Aggie, robbed the bank and hightailed it out of town."

"Money belong to ranchers," Crooked Grin said.

"The money that Sanders paid for the steers." A thought jumped into the sheriff's brain and it wouldn't go away.

He reined in his animal.

The others, seeing him stop, pulled up and turned in the saddle to face him. Tom slowly walked his horse towards them.

"Sheriff? You okay?" one of the men asked.

Tom was silent for while, the thought he'd had was beginning to make sense, but he needed to get it right in his head.

"Sheriff?"

"Yeah, yeah, I'm fine. Jus' give me a moment or two. I need to get my thoughts organized."

The men sat silently waiting for Tom to fill them in on what they were going to do.

"How long would it take to get round and approach the plateau from the northern end?" he asked Crooked Grin.

"One hour, maybe less. Why?"

"Then let's go," Tom said. He didn't want to voice his suspicions yet, but if the two men and Locklin were headed towards the plateau from the south, maybe, just maybe, it would be better to ride along the plateau from the north.

Once more, they set off at a gallop.

★ ★ ★

Bore and Dent reached the outcrop and dismounted. Unaware they were being pursued, they took time out for a smoke, before climbing up the slope towards the hidey-hole Dent had used to stash the money.

As they neared the hole, they both

197

heard the raucus from above.

"Shit, man!" Dent said. "I plum forgot 'bout the li'le lady."

"Hell, I ain't," Bore said. "We got time?"

"Nope. How long d'you think it'll be afore the town finds the bank's robbed and the manager's dead?" Dent asked.

"Hell, I dunno," Bore said. "Maybe with the storm an' all, a few more hours."

"You shit-fer-brains. The bank shoulda opened — " Dent took his pocketwatch out " — ten minutes ago. Don't you think they got some inklin' by now? An' if the town has, an' if what that Sanders fella said is true 'bout some o' his men watchin' out fer us, don't you think that we'll have a posse and Sanders' men out to git our hides nailed up?"

Bore thought about this: "I 'spose."

"You 'spose, well glory be. Let's jus' take the money an' run. I promise you this, soon as we reach another town, we can buy as many women as we can take. An' that's a fact."

Bore's face split open in a wide grin as that idea filled his head. "What're we waitin' fer?" he said, "let's git to it."

Meanwhile, above them on the plateau, the vultures dined out amid a frenzy of slashing beaks and claws.

13

AGGIE had long since ignored the slashing and clashing of beaks. She had become inured to it.

At first the sound of flesh being ripped from Charlie's body had made her want to vomit. The only reason she didn't was the thought of herself choking to death and the same scene being played out on her dead body.

With an inner strength she thought she'd all but used up, Aggie continued to roll away from Charlie's body until the sounds had diminished — not disappeared, they'd never do that — but she was far enough away now to cope with it.

She was still, now. Lying on her side, getting her breath back once again. She opened her eyes and saw the black, dust-covered boots standing inches from her head.

She closed her eyes again, thinking they'd come back to either kill or rape her; either way, she didn't care any more. She just hoped it'd be over quickly.

"Aggie?"

Aggie recognized the voice, but in her torment, she couldn't remember who it belonged to. Slowly, she opened her eyes once more. The boots had disappeared and in their place was the smiling, but worried-looking face of Clem Watkins.

He leaned forwards and untied the gag. Aggie took in huge gulps of hot air and then tried to lick her lips.

"Hold on now," Clem said. "Let's get these here ropes off."

Taking out a knife — he couldn't see the sense in prolonging her agony any longer than was necessary — he cut through the ropes used to fasten the sacking round her body, and then the bonds at her hands and feet. His heart ached and he winced slightly when he saw the raw sores where the ropes had burned in. She sure had put up a struggle to free herself, Clem thought.

Relief flooded through Aggie's hands and feet; she knew what would follow, but she didn't care.

Clem stood and reached for the canteen hanging loose on his saddle. Taking a handkerchief from his pocket, he soaked it in water and began to bath Aggie's forehead, then he dabbed water gently on her lips.

Aggie's mind said: "Thank you," but the word came out as a croak.

"There, there, Aggie, you jus' lie still now," Clem said as he let a few drops of water drip into Aggie's open mouth.

Aggie coughed, then Clem poured a few drops more into her mouth.

"You able to sit a-whiles?" he asked her gently.

Aggie nodded.

Clem put his arm behind her head and, sparing more his blushes than hers, he pulled her torn dress across her breasts.

"Who's that yonder?" he asked.

"Ch — ch — char — " Aggie couldn't say the name.

"Old Charlie?"

Aggie nodded.

"You reckon you can sit in my saddle? If'n you can, we're gonna get the hell out of here an' back to town."

Again, Aggie nodded.

Lifting her gently onto his horse, Clem began to lead the animal across the plateau.

★ ★ ★

Locklin reined in and watched as the two men he'd been looking for began to climb the slope. Half way up, they stopped and began sifting through a small bush. Locklin took out his spyglass and watched as, one by one, money-bags were placed on the bare rock.

Locklin dismounted, put his spyglass away and took out his Winchester. This was going to be like shooting pigs in a barrel, he thought.

He loosed off the first shot and the explosion echoed as if a thousand bullets had ripped into the silence of the desert air.

Bore, with his back to Locklin, looked down as blood and gore jumped out of his stomach.

He didn't say a word. A look of mild surprise registered on his face and he slumped forward, into the hole that minutes before held the answer to his dreams.

Dent, also taken by surprise, took awhiles before he ducked down behind the dead body of his pard. He quickly scanned the area and his eyes locked on Locklin's. He took out his sideiron, but he already knew it was useless. The Colt wouldn't even reach the man standing by the bay horse.

A cold sweat spread across Dent's forehead and gradually down his back and chest. He could neither move upwards or downwards and the man down on the desert floor could pick him off any time he chose.

Dent froze.

★ ★ ★

The shot was heard by Tom Hilks and the posse as they raced down the trail. God, he thought, I hope we ain't too late. They reached the north end of the plateau and had to slow down their speed as the hooves hit solid rock. Ahead, Tom saw a lone figure leading a horse with a rider walking towards them.

They reined in and took out their rifles.

"Hold it! Right there, mister," Tom shouted, down on one knee and sighting down the barrel of his rifle.

The figure waved, showing both hands in the air. "Tom?" the voice called out.

Tom lowered the hammer on his gun

and stared into the sunlight.

"Who's callin' my name?" he yelled.

"It's me. Clem, Clem Watkins. I done found Aggie!"

"Clem," Tom yelled back and began running towards man and horse.

He reached them, breathless, fearing the worst, but he saw that Aggie, although in a bad way, was alive.

She smiled as she saw Tom and he took her in his arms.

She winced as he hugged her.

"I'm sorry, I'm so sorry," he said. "Can you get her back to town, Clem?"

"That's where we're headed," Clem answered.

"Be careful, I've got some unfinished business to take care of."

Clem nodded, and, despite her discomfort, Aggie smiled at Tom and whispered, croakily: "Be careful."

Tom smiled and said he sure would — now.

Giving Clem his own horse, he told his men to leave theirs and follow him. Ahead, the plateau ended and the slope to the desert floor began. From their position, they couldn't see a dang thing, so they edged forward.

"Keep your heads down and wait for my orders," Tom whispered.

They reached the edge of the rock and, spread out, they peered down the slope.

Out in the desert, they saw the lone rider. Behind him came another rider, Tom couldn't make out the man, but he recognized Locklin.

Scanning the slope, he saw Jasper Dent and the money bags.

"Spread out," he whispered, "We got ourselves a murderin' bank robber."

★ ★ ★

Doug Sanders reached Chance Locklin just as Tom spread the posse along the edge of the plateau.

"What's goin' on?" Sanders demanded.

"Them two fellas you hired, *Mr* Sanders, they's up there and so's the money."

"Excellent!" Sanders enthused. "So, what're you waiting for? Go and get them."

"I'm still tryin' to figure out if'n you was setting me up, or them," Locklin said.

"Them, you idiot! Now go get my money!" Sanders was becoming annoyed.

"No one calls me an idiot, *Mr* Sanders. Not even you!"

"Then stop actin' like one. Now I gave you an order!"

Locklin, still with his Winchester cocked and ready, levelled the barrel and, with a grin on his face, gently squeezed the trigger.

Just before the hammer hit home, Sanders realized what was about to happen. He reached for his gun, but it was too late.

The slug, fired from only two feet, sent Sanders flying backwards through the air, landing some six feet away from where he stood.

The man was stone dead.

"Hellfire!" Tom said as he recognized the besuited figure of Sanders die in front of his eyes. He then watched as Locklin turned his attention back to Dent.

"Throw the money down, Dent, an' I might let you live!"

"Go to hell," Dent replied. "You want it, you come and get it!"

Locklin, cock-sure, began to approach the rocky slope. As Dent hadn't fired back, Locklin was sure he hadn't got a rifle. He confirmed this as he reached the two horses, Winchesters still in their scabbards.

Smiling once more, Locklin began to climb up the slope. He knew how accurate a sideiron was and roughly the distance it could shoot relatively straight, and he was well outside that.

Dent watched him approach: Come on, just a few more feet, he thought, just a few more feet and maybe I'll get lucky.

Locklin knew exactly what he was doing. He was gambling on Dent taking the risk of standing to shoot it out. He was a smart poker player, and his gamble paid off.

Dent could wait no longer. Sweat was pouring off him as he decided that Locklin was close enough. He jumped to his feet and fired off six shots in close succession. As the sixth shot was loosed off, Locklin, firing the Winchester from the hip, squeezed his trigger — once.

Dent slammed back into the rocky slope — dead.

Locklin waited a few moments before he continued his unhurried climb up the slope. He checked both bodies by kicking them hard and, satisfied both men were dead, he began picking up the money bags. There were more than he could handle in one trip, so he began tossing them down the slope; one by one they tumbled. The last two he carried with him.

Tom and the posse watched and waited. Slowly, they too, edged forwards. When Tom saw the man's back, both hands full, and the man's rifle tucked under one arm, he made his move.

Standing, he yelled: "Hold it right there, mister!"

Locklin stood rock still.

"Drop the bags an' the rifle and throw your sideiron where I can see it."

Locklin didn't move a muscle.

"You hear me, mister?" Tom called out.

Locklin turned slowly: he saw the badge on the man's vest.

"Howdy, Sheriff," he said slowly. Locklin was gambling again. Gambling the man wouldn't shoot him dead.

"I said drop the bags an' the rifle. Do it!"

"Well, Sheriff, I don't know that I can do that," Locklin said lazily, trying to lull the sheriff.

"If'n you don't," Tom yelled, losing his patience, "you're a dead man. Now *drop those bags!*"

Locklin made his move.

Letting the bags fall from his hands,

the rifle slid into them in one easy movement. He knew there was a slug in the breach and he squeezed the trigger.

A dozen shots rang out as Tom and the rest of the posse fired as one. Locklin shot backwards through the air and tumbled to the foot of the slope.

Tom removed his Stetson and mopped his brow. If his bullets had hit Locklin, then he'd killed his first man.

Slowly, the posse made their way carefully down the slope, guns levelled, even though they all knew there was no one but them left alive.

★ ★ ★

Sadie was in the bedroom with Aggie. She'd been bathed and her arms and legs bandaged. All she needed now was rest, and she'd get plenty of that.

"So how come you knew?" Harold Meeks asked Tom as the two men sat drinking a cool beer in the front parlour.

"I don't know, Harold. It just came like a bolt out of the blue. Everything that went on seemed to be linked up in some way with Sanders. I didn't know it all, though. Not 'til I had a chat with one of the men who rode with Locklin. He sure filled me in on a whole bunch of stuff.

"Then, suddenly, everything fell into place: the shootings, Sanders' presence in town, the money, the bank being robbed.

"Sanders planned to have the bank robbed by Locklin and his gang, that's why they came into town the night of the storm. He didn't figure on Dent and Bore beating him to it.

"Sanders had hired Dent and Bore to rob the bank that he'd already *had* robbed, he'd then make sure they got caught in the act. That way, he'd be out on the trail an' in the clear.

"Aggie was the fly in the ointment." Tom paused, taking in a mouthful of beer. "If Dent and Bore hadn't've kidnapped her, he might've got away with it."

"An' Charlie?" Harold asked.

"Poor ol' Charlie was jus' in the wrong place at the wrong time. That's all. Sanders wanted the steers *and* the money he was due to hand out to the drovers and the ranchers. Stupid thing is, he'd've made a handsome profit on the steers alone." Tom handed a sheet of neatly folded paper to Harold.

From the Office of
The Chief of Police
Los Angeles, California
To Sheriff Tom Hilks,
Woebegone, California

Sheriff Hilks,

I thank you for your enquiry regarding a certain Douglas Sanders.

Yes, we are very familiar with this man and have been watching him for many weeks now.

Any information you can supply will

greatly help the case we are building up on him.

He and a certain Mexican, Miguel Fernandez, have cornered the market in beef sales in Los Angeles. That, and prostitution, murder and extortion. We're pretty close now to arresting Mr Sanders.

Hope this information is helpful to you, we shall be in touch in a few weeks when Mr Sanders returns to Los Angeles.

Yours faithfully
(on behalf of)
Chief of Police
James T. Cooper

"Seems a man like that deserved all he got," Harold said when he'd read the letter.

"Well, he sure got it," Tom said. Both men drained their glasses just as Aggie called out.

"Tom? Tom, are you still here?"

"Coming," Tom said and ran through to the bedroom.

"I'm still here and I ain't *ever* gonna leave you." He sat on the side of the bed and they kissed.

Sadie backed out of the bedroom and, silently, she closed the door.

THE END